LUCINIE

A Novel

A Novel

LUCINIE

BY

M. L. PASCAL DASQUE

P. J. Kenedy & Sons
New York

LUCINIE

is a translation of a novel of the same title
by M. L. Pascal Dasque (Paris: Spes, 1958)

Library of Congress Catalog Card Number: 59–12897

To My Mother

Chapter I

A LOW WINDOW opened brown shutters on the silent street of the Algerian town where the houses, their even fronts reflecting the sunlight, had maintained from the beginnings of the colony an air of gentle impersonality. Only the small newsboy dared to make his presence known about eight in the morning by a single call. Then he crept silently from door to door, sliding a copy of the same newspaper under each, and not renewing his yells until he had turned the corner into Alexandria Street.

To the northeast, the first room of the convent overlooked the entrance hall, and through a narrow arched door one could reach a big, irregular-shaped room where an old empire clock tick-tocked, and pass to the kitchen and refectory. Sister Dominique liked to use it as her parlor and laundry. Long beams of light filtering through the slats of the shaded window lighted up a portrait of the Pope and an ebony crucifix behind which was stuck a dried-out olive branch on the other wall. On summer afternoons the Mother Superior raised the sash to let some fresh air blow on the white wooden table and into the inner courtyard.

She would bring her linen basket here to patch or sew, or even iron. Formerly she did this task in the kitchen by the coal stove, but she preferred to work in the front reception room, where she could keep an eye simultaneously on the outer door and on the preparation of the meals. This was how she kept the convent in balance. Occasionally she took a book and read for a while in the library, but since winter her work had left not a single free moment. The other nuns were so busy on outside work for the sick every day for the last five months that they could not help.

This afternoon Sister Dominique's head was bent over a linen front belonging to Sister Pélagie which she was mending. In the intensity of her application to the task she pouted out her lower lip, accentuating its thickness and ugliness. The young woman would protest when she found out, but the Mother Superior was not prepared to let her add this chore to her crowded schedule. Apart from Sister St. Jean, who was forever moaning about her problems and Sister Anne of the Cross, the convent numbered only four young sisters, all from Europe, and all exhausted by a particularly trying work load and by an early start of the heat of summer which was already crushing them. Only last evening when she got back Sister Pélagie had relaxed by soaking her skinny arms in a basin of water to cool off, and Sister Dominique re-called quite clearly the paleness of those frail members.

She sighed. She, too, felt all the weight of this cruel period of summer heat, but what troubled her more than their common physical tiredness was the spiritual lassitude of the community. She lacked the ability to do her job well. She knew that she was perfectly competent to look after the material progress of the convent, to supervise the work of each of the nuns, and to see to their health. But because she herself had leaned heavily on her own superiors and had always got from them the help she needed, she doubted her ability as a guide of souls. Her natural timidity and her difficulty in expressing herself made this role distasteful just as much as did her feeling of inferiority. And this emotional attitude even prevented her from asserting herself and imposing her will on the community. She had not succeeded in eliminating the atmosphere of fear, ill humor, and even hostility created by Sister St. Jean.

Sister Dominique did not have the courage to deal severely with this companion, twenty years her elder, whose surly, malevolent, suspicious character kept the convent in disorder. For a long time Sister St. Jean had known how to escape discipline, and as she grew older she freed herself further from authority, while always finding new ways to impose her judgment and her whims on others. The Mother Superior preferred to console Sister St. Jean's victims rather than challenge the aggressor directly, a technique motivated by gentleness and by a deep faith that blindly believed the wisdom and natural goodness of the members of her order.

Nevertheless, she could not continue to hide from herself the fact that this indulgence was aggravating the old sister's defects, and that her demoralizing influence was magnified by the fatigue of the other five sisters to a point where it threatened the very life of the convent. The damage did not reveal itself in a revolt or in complaints, but rather in a general silence, a tendency of each to isolate herself, a slackening of devotion sensed rather than identified. The sisters were even losing control over their reactions. Several days ago Sister Jeanne had broken a plate, and that evening there had been a noticeable and irritating scraping and scratching of chairs as from time to time they were moved about on the chapel floor.

Sister Dominique picked up Sister Lucinie's cap. This nun caused the Mother Superior her greatest doubts. What would she be able to say about her when she reported on her term of office, during her summer trip to the motherhouse? A letter from the Mother General had come with this young woman. "I want you," it said, "to bear in mind Sister Lucinie's extreme youth and gloss over an occasional outburst of enthusiasm. I am entrusting to you a very sensitive nun, and I believe her moral worth goes far beyond what one finds in the average sister. But this sensitivity runs the risk of becoming the stumbling block on which such fine promise may shatter . . . "

Sister Dominique thought that the Mother General never made a mistake. Nevertheless, her own observation had failed to confirm the existence of either the unhealthy sensitivity to which the letter had drawn her attention or the spiritual potential the importance of which it had stressed. She had found only a laughing child, perhaps a little frivolous, but a good companion and an excellent nurse. And so her fears had dissolved. More recently, however, the evolution of Sister Lucinie's character had raised new doubts. Sister Dominique dated this change from January 6, the morning on which the young woman had indulged in her last childish prank.

The series of epidemics that shortly afterward overwhelmed the town had not yet begun. It was the feast of the Epiphany, and only Sister Perpétue was away from the convent. Sister Lucinie spent the morning arranging sheets in the large wardrobe on the first floor. She loved this work. However, it occupied much time and little effort, so that her energetic temperament accumulated in her excessive reserves of activity and dreams.

"Reverend Mother," she remarked, as Sister Dominique passed beside her, "we can thank Sister Jeanne's loving care for a shining stairway perfumed with wax. See how this heavy wooden banister now fits the hand placed on it, how these narrow steps call for the foot of the story-book princess. Close your eyes and you will hear her royal highness trip lightly past.

"And today," she added with a smile, as the two of them reached the foot of the stairs together, "the wise kings from the East adore their Lord, and I, daughter and spouse of the King, am a princess in a gown with trailing skirt, my black veil transformed into a high headdress lost in a cloud of lace and embroidery, my rosary beads a golden chain and my linen neckband a collar of ermine."

Sister Lucinie laughed and pirouetted about the

11

Mother Superior, who was both shocked and amused. But Sister St. Jean shot like a whirlwind from the kitchen. Sister Dominique preferred not to recall the scandalous scene, yet could not forget the cruel blue eyes, the livid face, the tightly squeezed lips, bloodless and screwed out of shape by the virulent rebukes the old nun showered on Sister Lucinie with total disregard for the dignity of the convent.

The Mother Superior shivered as she recalled the innocent face of the young woman, at first astonished and laughing, then gradually turning a brilliant red and finally changing to a blue-gray pallor; her utter silence; the fear that slowly took possession of her and filled her two big eyes. Sister Dominique had been unable to calm the old nun, but Sister Anne of the Cross finally found a way to end the scene. She took Sister Lucinie by the hand and led her to the Superior. "Child," she said with affectionate gentleness, "you owe Reverend Mother an apology."

Sister Dominique felt, as did the others, that the young woman had been guilty of no fault. Nevertheless, she admired Sister Anne of the Cross's technique for pacifying Sister St. Jean by appearing to agree with her while at the same time softening the humiliation for Sister Lucinie by having her apologize only to the Mother Superior and by reassuring her frightened companion with gentle words.

The meal that followed was a dreary one. Sister St. Jean felt, possibly for the first time, the disapproval of the community. Ashamed, she hid her chagrin in a total silence. Sister Lucinie seemed lost in a gloomy dream from which her companions' kind attentions could not free her. From then on she had lived an introverted life despite the urging of the Mother Superior and the tongue-lashings of Sister St. Jean, who considered this withdrawal a personal insult and resented it bitterly.

Chapter II

SISTER ST. JEAN was the first to return home, but instead of stopping, as usual, to greet Sister Dominique, she went straight to her cell. The community always kept the easiest tasks for her. From time to time, however, she insisted on undertaking a particularly difficult assignment, not from any spirit of penance, but to be able to complain afterward and make a show of her exhaustion, both in the convent and outside, thus providing herself with a very useful instrument of moral torture to use both against her juniors and her Superior.

From earliest childhood she had always played the role of scourge, filled with a sense of her own right to direct, to dictate, and to oppress. After the flame of the novitiate years, during which faith had covered over her

14

authoritarian tendencies, humility had gradually withered in step with the decline in her desire to become a saint. She was now just a poor old nun with no real authority other than that which she exercised over that foolish Sister Dominique.

Sister St. Jean repeated three times the phrase "poor old nun," and tears rolled down her fat cheeks. She could open up this torrent of self-pity whenever she wanted. It gave her some pleasure, a tonic that enabled her to think more every day about the ingratitude of others and about the persecution of which she felt herself the object. The post of Mother Superior always escaped her, and yet of all the sisters she believed that she alone had the qualifications for it. With the sole exception of Sister Lucinie, she was better educated than any of them. Sister Dominique wrote correctly and knew how to spell, but her handwriting was heavy and childish and she read the Latin prayers very badly. Even little Sister Perpétue, who came from a working-class family of the port of Bizerta, made a better fist of it than she did. As for Sister Anne of the Cross, after forty years as a nun she had never gotten away from a spontaneity and earthiness of expression that came out, even when she spoke about the most spiritual matters, in a shocking way. Sister Pélagie lacked a grade-school certificate. And that left only Sister Jeanne.

Sister St. Jean loved to dig deep into the most trivial details of the lives of others and almost always found a way to satisfy her intense curiosity, but Sister Jeanne's reserve was a stone wall. The only conclusions Sister St. Jean could draw were those revealed by studying the other's behavior; it seemed to her that the young nun

15

took such pleasure in housekeeping that she must have the soul of a domestic servant.

Sister St. Jean was satisfied that her own religion was more spiritual than that of the others. She could sincerely tell herself that she sought nothing other than God, her ability to reject in words every material desire enabling her to enjoy that tainted pleasure of which she publicly boasted. All her actions were designed to impress others. She could never be alone in any true sense. Even in her own room behind closed doors she peopled the space in her imagination with an audience which — according to her mood — admired, expressed astonishment, or suffered torments.

Her openly indicated desire to head the community did not seem to her blameworthy or contradictory. She sought no honor but only the service of God. Of course in her daydreams she gave herself over to self-admiration, delighting in the impression she would make on her companions, on the other people of her home town, and on the members of her family, but all this dream life she simply put to one side when she was dealing with God. Besides, she dealt with Him as she would with anyone who came to see her. She kept for Him at a certain time a smiling part of her soul, and when occasionally she went to the length of asking His help to perform some insignificant undertaking, the emotion with which she formulated her prayer prevented her understanding her weakness. The old nun thought more highly of her own formal behavior than of the simple faith of her companions and their daily offering of their lives to the Most High, as though He really lowered Himself by maintaining constant relations with Sister Dominique's

16

timid scruples, the jokes perpetrated by Sister Anne of the Cross, Sister Perpétue's medals, Sister Pélagie's weakness, and Sister Jeanne's secrets. And even if it was not quite clear that Sister Lucinie would go to hell, God, in any case, would keep an insignificant place for this daughter of upper middle-class parents who was so obvious in her efforts to lower herself to the level of ordinary mortals.

In a word, Sister St. Jean was the member of the community with the most highly developed sense of initiative and the worldly resourcefulness that immediately enables a convent to form part of the society around it. Sister Dominique did not behave as befitted a lady, neglected courtesy visits to the important families of the town, refused to join in drawing-room conversations of the kind that made Mother St. Augustine of the St. Louis Institution famous, even excused herself from performing the role of director of consciences which so became the Mother Superior of the Puimerol Clinic. Sister Dominique sat with folded hands at a level below that for which she was destined, and Sister St. Jean went on happily dreaming about the changes she would make in the convent when she became acting head during the summer while the Superior was away.

Chapter III

SISTER ANNE of the Cross sank into a chair beside the Mother Superior. After the customary exchange
of greetings, she devoted her entire attention to relaxing,
an amused smile on her thin lips, her eyelids, with their
scanty eyelashes, half-closed in a malicious expression.
She wanted to rest a few minutes in silence, yet not too
long. The words were building up inside her, and when
this happened, she could not hold them back. She took
life in a rather droll way and found it absolutely necessary to tell somebody whatever she happened to be thinking. But she also had to draw her breath. She was getting
old, and she had just completed a trying errand at high
speed.

She took the mended linens, amusing herself by separating them into small packages, one for each nun.

"You," she grumbled, "are preparing for yourself four waves of complaints, not to mention mine, since you have done nothing for me. You are using your eyes for the young, while I, who soon won't have a pair of stockings to wear because I don't have time to darn them, am reduced to envying the others. You must recognize your exclusive responsibility for this sin."

Sister Dominique laid two pairs of stockings hidden in the fold of her habit on her companion's knees, and the pair laughed happily, enjoying the pleasure of rediscovering how close to each other they remained in body and mind. These surprises, no longer such because so often repeated, these pretended complaints had become a kind of ritual, a life they made for themselves apart from the others so that they could behave in the childish fashion of their youth. Sister Anne of the Cross found it easier to enter this make-believe world and always succeeded in quieting the doubts which the Mother Superior sometimes entertained regarding the propriety of their behavior.

"Come to think of it," she would say, "how could we ever forgive Sister Perpétue, if we were not a little like her ourselves?"

Sister Dominique never lost her self-control because of the jests of the young nuns, as did the intolerant Sister St. Jean, but her patience resulted from a long interior struggle, and not, like that of Sister Anne of the Cross, from a natural disposition. Her acceptance reflected an element of indifference, for her laugh never had the hearty ring of that of the younger woman. It retained the quality it had when she was a child. This

19

she understood, and she could restrain and estimate the effects, though she never fully entered into the emotion of the others and to some extent distrusted it. She was unlike Sister Anne of the Cross in that she lacked the gift of penetrating and recognizing the feelings of others. No doubt she had a quick intuition for sensing the mood of her companions, but she never dared join in their happiness or attempted to comfort them, being unable to distinguish the sources from which their sorrows or their joys sprang. Sister Anne of the Cross cured souls as easily as bodies. She had a better understanding of temperamental differences, and, in consequence, the vivacity of her pleasantries and her optimism permitted her to achieve a happy and amused serenity which the Mother Superior seemed unable to find. Perhaps Sister Anne of the Cross did not know the purer forms of truth, so that the effect of her message was merely to reduce the wildest dreams and the deepest sorrows to more modest dimensions and to remind man of his humanity. But this ability and this limited truth were in practice extremely useful, giving each recipient a sense of equilibrium and safety.

For the moment she went over the day's incidents with Sister Dominique. Her assignment for some time was a considerable distance away, but her work entailed fewer problems than usual because she was nursing in a family where she was spared all housekeeping duties. She seemed strong in spite of her tiny figure, and not nearly so tired as the younger nuns.

In the room above them, they could hear Sister St. Jean moving about, and the noise reminded Sister Anne of the Cross of her companion's trifling gossip. For a

20

moment she looked with pity on the worried old face of the Mother Superior, the thick mouth, the long jaws, and the big nose — an ugly face, no doubt, yet free of the vulgarity that Sister St. Jean attributed to it. The gentleness of the glance and the lack of self-assurance gave it a spiritual character which at times covered up the unattractive elements. Sister Anne did not like to see those eyes cloud with worry, as they did with every new problem, and nevertheless she felt obliged to add to Sister Dominique's troubles.

"Tomorrow," she said, "I want to take Sister Pélagie's place. Don't look at me like that. I asked you before never to give Sister St. Jean too much opportunity for private conversation with any of the young nuns. In spite of that, Sister Pélagie leaves with her every morning as they go to work. I can't say with absolute certainty that she gives bad advice to our daughters, but she tends to belittle our Order and flashes the attractions of life in the world before them. The children are defenseless against attacks made with such skill that they seem to stress the importance of our work. Instead of suggesting that our existence is empty, she will say: 'We know nothing of the world's pleasures and escape motherhood, but we accept all of that for God, because our life is devoted to His service and we have chosen the better part.' Then she will add: 'Nevertheless, those who claim that it is more natural to follow the trend of the world are not wrong. One must have a superior personality to perform the obligations of the religious state properly, and in my opinion it is better to make a good mother than a bad nun. For my own part, if I had ever felt at any time during my life that a doubt existed within me, I

21

should have preferred to take off the habit and go back home.' "

A moment of silence was broken only by Sister St. Jean's steps upstairs.

"You understand," continued Sister Anne of the Cross, "that when she speaks of home, she thinks of her village. She has never really established herself emotionally as one of us, and she makes the young sisters feel that they are living among strangers, that the convent does not belong to them, that they are merely passing through. She takes all the humanity out of the religious life, placing it on a peak which few could hope to scale. Naturally these children, on whom we have been impressing the virtue of humility, think it would be quite impossible for them to reach such a height, and just as naturally, after raising the doubt, she suggests the escape."

"But why?" Sister Dominique demanded.

She had stopped sewing and sat listening in a mood of despair, her two hands on her knees, a needle in one and a big ball of black cotton in the other.

"She wants to see your administration shipwrecked, hoping that thus she can replace you."

Sister Dominique said nothing. What she had just heard swirled around inside her like a storm. She was waiting for a terrific thunder clap that would destroy her. She even relished the idea. It would mean an end to her problems here below and take her direct to paradise. But no cataclysm occurred, beyond the sensation of burning and choking in her lungs and this whirling of her thoughts in her brain which made her feel a wreck.

In her sorrow she felt the need to pray, to reflect in

22

isolation before judging and making a decision. She suspected that Sister Anne of the Cross was unintentionally exaggerating, and in consequence placing Sister St. Jean's acts in a false perspective. Yet if by any chance her companion was not deceived, then it was her duty to take immediate action against the old nun and protect the community.

For the third time Sister St. Jean moved about above their heads. The Mother Superior decided that she should assert her authority fully, and that at least for some days she should avoid any appearance of friendliness, even toward Sister Anne of the Cross. Her convent was in danger. The thing to do was to strengthen the observance of the rule and exact the maximum response from each nun. She got to her feet, indicating with an almost imperceptible sign that she wanted her companion to do the same.

"The offense against me is of no account," she declared in a hoarse voice. "I have always forgiven it, and indeed that was easy. I believe, however, that certain cases call for punishment, first of all in the interest of the guilty party, and then to protect the victims. The law of pardon does not exclude severity, and I shall attend to that.

"Nevertheless, an accusation of the kind you have made cannot be accepted without reflection. I shall ask God to advise me. I want you to take charge of the work in the kitchen until Sister Lucinie arrives, and then take a rest. You will call me at seven. And whatever decision I may shortly make, I ask you to avoid from this moment all contact with Sister St. Jean."

The outside door opened silently and Sister Lucinie

entered, followed by Sister Pélagie. Sister Dominique made a sign to her old friend to leave.

"Dear Sister Pélagie," she ordered dryly, "a few minutes of prayer would be good for your soul. Your companion can prepare the meal and lay the table."

She passed between them, leaving her work on the table, while the two astonished young women hesitated, their eyes on the hunched shoulders, the strange, harsh voice ringing in their ears.

With difficulty the Mother Superior bent her arthritic knees, waiting until Sister Pélagie, a seat behind her and vaguely visible to the right out of the corner of her eye, also knelt. Then she began to pray. Sister Pélagie had not quite closed the chapel door, and she did not dare either to make her go back or humiliate her by doing so herself. The slight noises of the quiet house disturbed her troubled mind and prevented her from recalling just what had happened. She heard the light step as Sister Lucinie went down toward the office, the bottle of milk being emptied, and the water faucet opening. In spite of herself, the comings and goings of the housekeeper and her familiar actions blended before her eyes with Sister St. Jean's movements. Then she heard Sister Perpétue come in, followed her quick steps along the passage into the reception room and on to the kitchen, and heard her astonished question: "Where is Reverend Mother?"

The detail eased her pain. The friendly tone of the question, as well as her recollection of the first reaction of Sisters Pélagie and Lucinie, reaffirmed that the nuns loved her, and — as Sister Anne's warning also indicated — that they respected in her the Superior. Sister Jeanne

24

would probably arrive in the same way and her first concern would be to salute her.

Sister Dominique's guilt in allowing Sister St. Jean to go on behaving so badly resulted from her lack of submission to the judgment of the Mother General who in appointing her to her post had made a choice the wisdom of which she herself had dared to criticize as much from true humility as because Sister St. Jean's opinion weighed with her more than that of the Mother General. Now, she understood that strict obedience would have been better than her scruples and her partial rejection of the role of spiritual advisor which her position demanded. Reflecting thus on her own case, she gained a better idea of the extent of Sister St. Jean's corrosive influence on the souls of the others, and began to wonder what still-unrevealed havoc might have been wrought on Sister Pélagie. She felt the need to question the young woman right away, but when she looked, the young nun's eyes were fixed on the altar and she was deep in meditation. Unsure of herself, the Mother Superior returned to her reflections, allowing the peace of prayer to soak into the bowed figures.

The silent gesture almost lost in the half-darkness sufficed, nevertheless, to attract the other nun's attention, and she turned her head slightly. Sister Dominique, however, had resumed her former attitude and Sister Pélagie looked back again at the tiny altar covered with a snow-white cloth on which Sister Lucinie had embroidered some roses. For a moment she let her fancy follow the dancing reflection of the candle flame on the tabernacle's ornaments until her heavy, sleep-filled eyes began to droop.

Only a while ago the journey back in the bright afternoon and Sister Dominique's anger, complementing the effect of the fresh air, had dispelled the sleep that had been crushing Sister Pélagie since midday. But now in the half-darkness and the heavy, still atmosphere of the chapel, her tiredness returned to overwhelm her, and she had to fight the temptation to rest her head on her joined hands and fall asleep where she knelt. She could not even continue to pray, experiencing a sudden distress when she realized how poorly she resisted the urges of her body, no less than those of her mind and heart. Unpleasant dreams began to form themselves in her mind, their power over her strengthened by her drowsiness, so that she was only half-conscious of what was happening. The only thought that remained was that she must not violate the conventions by dozing off.

She had been a nun for eight years. She had first turned toward God from an unhappy love affair, but during the years of her novitiate she had let all bitterness subside in her and be replaced by the love of Christ. After these first years of service, since her transfer to this convent, her affection for God, while not weakening or lessening, had nevertheless allowed her former lover to become again gradually more important, so that in course of time she had become wrapped up in this memory. A strange thing, however, happened. Each time she recalled him the outline became less precise. And so she ended up adoring God, but loving with tender affection an imaginary being endowed by her with a chimerical life and appearance, investing him with the poetic atmosphere of the prince charming of her youthful fairy tales. These two conflicting trends coexisted within her, each harming the other, disturbing the tranquillity of her relations with God by taking quick possession of her and undermining her ability to fight them. In consequence, the young woman lived in dread of the eternal damnation that her faith warned her was in store whenever her imaginary lover appeared.

This fuzzy image, or rather this thought, had reached the point of being habitually present. It entered her mind while she prayed, returned while she was talking to someone, when she was settling to sleep, during her daily tasks. Indeed it had become a second life. It was now no longer a lover who came to meet her. It was rather that she had become the lover and as such thought as a lover about herself. She had become a man who loved the girl she herself had been with that lightsome, musical, ill-defined love which she had desired in her romantic youth. And at the same time the nun still lived in her, carrying out her duties of charity and humility. Each day, however, she sank deeper into a dangerous softness, neglecting her meditations, sullying her prayers with the unsought return of the fictitious person, and finally widening the breach by incomplete and badly presented confessions.

All of this lowered her own opinion of herself, and without giving her the courage she needed for a struggle she might easily have won, overwhelmed her with a weakness and self-contempt that destroyed all hope of gaining God. The difficulty of salvation, as presented to her by Sister St. Jean, had completed the collapse and broken down her last faint desire to continue the struggle. She

27

felt that all the virtues she formerly had practiced and all the remorse that had failed to make her renounce her dream could not compensate for the evil she was causing, so that at times she was seized with a great temptation to renounce God, abandon everything, and let herself be carried away by this other being as by a tidal wave.

A hand rested lightly on her and she heard Sister Perpétue's gentle laughter ring in her ears: "Wake up, Sister Pélagie, wake up. Reverend Mother is waiting for you." With a pang she jerked herself erect, ashamed at having fallen asleep.

"You are simply worn out," the little nun whispered. "This heat is crushing us, especially those of you who come from the north. If only we could spare enough time for a good rest."

It came as a new surprise to Sister Pélagie each time to hear the other nuns frankly confess their weakness. She could never bring herself to such candor, managing to keep herself afloat only by hiding her failings, and compelled, in consequence, to live up to the impression that her companions had of her.

Before coming to the convent she had built a concept of stainless purity about monastic life, and only her faith in her own youth and strength had enabled her to believe that she could ever hope to live such a life. The few years in the motherhouse had chased these illusions away. The life seemed much less difficult than she had anticipated and was lived on less dizzy peaks, yet her temperament was such that she could not follow this reality without occasional deviations. She had a sweet tooth she could not always control. Besides, she had trouble in concentrating wholeheartedly during meditation, and also in conquering her impatience.

It was a strange situation. She knew that she still had strength inside her, as much as before, but she now lacked the will to test it, to fire the first shot. Until quite recently she believed that one day she would force herself to fight and that she would win, but — and of course she did not realize that her physical tiredness was largely responsible for the moral weakening — she was beginning to contemplate a solution by default. This new attitude dated from a few weeks ago, specifically from an occasion on which Sister St. Jean had criticized her attitude.

"Sister Pélagie, do sit down."

Once again Sister Perpétue's voice brought her back to reality. She took her seat, surprised to find herself in the refectory among her companions. Though she had not heard the grace before meals being recited, her hands were joined in an attitude of recollection. "An automaton," she thought to herself despairingly. "I am nothing now but an automaton." Her whole face flushed red with humiliation, and in a flash she saw how sad and ugly she had made an existence she had wanted to be perfect.

Chapter IV

I T W A S Sister Dominique's turn. Once again she opened the book she held in her hands, her finger serving as a bookmark in the pages. She was entirely wrapped up in her prayer, so that without following the words on the paper she was able to continue the recitation. Nevertheless, the thoughts she had driven deep down into the bottom of her soul to be able to celebrate this afternoon before God with as much beauty as lay in her power, these sorrowful and anguished thoughts refused to be driven away entirely. Like a background to the chant of the community prayers she could hear their moans, and it troubled her.

Her missal smelled like an old book with an odor of incense. She already loved it although she had had it only a short time. She found it easier to make out the tall, fat letters than the small and faded ones of her old prayer book. This gift from the Superior General, she thought, made up for a long life of devotion and discipline, but she no longer deserved it because she was letting evil enter in among her nuns.

She began her part, but having once let remorse become mixed up for a moment in her prayer, she had opened the dikes and her troubles were now overwhelming all her emotions. She read mechanically, all these Latin words rising up in the little chapel where the seven women filled almost the entire available space. In silence, in the interior of each soul, the nuns repeated the words with mounting fervor. A great calm rose up in the half-lighted room from the prayer books that the hands enfolded in their whiteness, from the starched caps and the circular guimpes, from the chairs made of white straw. A cool breeze laden with perfume came in through the tiny window, at times wafting the smell of wax of the two lighted candles toward the nuns. The distant music of a party also reached them on the breeze, its rhythms softened by the distance and spiritualized by the night. The voice of the Superior and the droning of the responses sung in plain chant by the choir rose in turn, and at regular intervals the crinkling of pages turned in unison broke the rhythm.

A calm descended on each of the nuns, easing her extreme weariness and filling her heart with peace. Sister Perpétue even felt a great joy rise within her, and she laughed out loud because Sister Dominique fumbled a word and had to repeat it three times.

Her laughter broke the harmony and repose of the

chapel. Sister Anne of the Cross expressed her disapproval in a peremptory exclamation, and each one turned back to the concerns of her own soul. After a moment of deep silence the Superior stood up and the others followed her to the first floor. On the landing she stopped them before they had time to enter their respective cells.

"Sister Jeanne," she ordered, "tomorrow you will take Sister St. Jean's place and for the rest of the week you will be responsible for distributing the soup to the poor. In the afternoon you will go to look after Mademoiselle Reynaud," she added, turning to Sister St. Jean and catching the surprised look on her face.

The group broke up. Even Sister Anne of the Cross did not dare offer an opinion about this unexpected change announced at so late an hour. She was conscious of the presence of the protective severity which the Superior had mentioned to her that afternoon, and though she herself had provoked it, she was unable to avoid a sense of grievance. She felt that it was unfair to Sister St. Jean and all the young women who without exception felt themselves vaguely threatened by this unanticipated dissatisfaction, an attitude very hard to reconcile with Sister Dominique's ordinary gentleness.

Sister Jeanne and Sister St. Jean separated without daring to express to each other their concern except by a glance, and Sister Perpétue felt her joy die within her. Quickly her exhaustion returned and she decided to pass up the prayers she said each evening in her cell. She undressed and lay down, longing for the sleep which, after leaving her half incapacitated all day long, now refused to come. She shared neither the uneasy curiosity of her companions nor the fear that she might have merited the anger of the Superior, but a childish vexation and a need to weep prevented her from dwelling on any thought other than this threat confronting all the others. Fumblingly she looked for her rosary beads, began to say a decade, and fell asleep even before she had got to the end of it.

Chapter V

SISTER JEANNE knelt on the tiled floor, leaning her forehead on her hands, which in turn rested on the window sill. She recited an Our Father slowly, then began to reflect on the Mother Superior's decision. The change in her duties was not in itself remarkable. It often happened that an assignment was switched, either to utilize the community resources more efficiently or to avoid the development of an excessive attachment between the nursing sister and a patient's family. What was unusual about the decision just made was Reverend Mother's tone and the timing of the announcement.

Normally Sister Dominique gave notice to the nuns of their work for the following day before evening prayers, and she never spoke in severe tones. Sister Jeanne had thought her incapable of such harshness. The change was meant to punish someone, but who could the someone possibly be?

As she examined her conscience, Sister Jeanne found nothing in her own conduct to merit a penalty, but on the other hand she did not think that an old nun like Sister St. Jean could deserve to be called to order.

Sister Jeanne understood in a confused way that Sister St. Jean's behavior left not a little to be desired, but her conclusion was an intuitive one because she followed the gospel precept of never judging the conduct of others, confining herself to keeping away from those who seemed to her to lack peace of soul. This evening she recognized for the first time her mistrust of the old sister. She realized, however, that the mistrust had existed for some days, although she was not able to say precisely what had first given rise to it, and she went on immediately to tell herself that this irrational rejection and failure to examine the facts also involved some lack of charity.

Unless her avoidance of Sister St. Jean was based on concrete data, she told herself, her lack of confidence would be unjustified and would violate the law of love. Christ had indeed directed us not to condemn others, but the need to avoid temptations and sources of danger called for an objective viewpoint. A judgment, accordingly, had to be thought of as consisting of two elements, on the one hand the ability to distinguish, and on the other the attribution of blame or praise. It was this adoption of a position that Jesus had forbidden to His disciples. In the incident of the woman taken in adultery or in that of Mary Magdalene, He had not glossed over the faults of these two women as of no account, but He had refused to punish them. Distinguishing the sin from the person, He did not scorn the sinner but hated the evil. Indeed all His preaching had the single purpose of preventing it. He did not ask His followers to approve blindly the personal qualities of others, but simply to forgive their faults.

Sister Jeanne's reasoning thus led her to the conclusion that she should study Sister St. Jean if she would avoid doing her an injustice. Then, according to the decision at which she might arrive, she should either excuse her fault but continue to maintain her distance as a matter of self-protection, or she should break down her reserve and be sorry that she had wronged her companion.

What was it, she asked herself, that had urged her to withdraw from Sister St. Jean? A certain air of harshness, a too obvious bitterness about the mouth? That might possibly indicate a soul that lacked calm, but it proved nothing. An excessive tenseness in one's dealings with oneself and continued scrupulousness could destroy spiritual calm and alter the lines of the face. Her distrust came rather from the older woman's all-too-obvious anxiety to show off, her tendency to take advantage of the presence of others to undertake some difficult task, to perform a sacrifice or a fast, or to spend far more time than anybody else in making the Way of the Cross in the chapel.

No sooner had Sister Jeanne formulated this grievance in her mind than she felt ashamed of herself. Should she criticize the poor old nun for excessive piety? Sister Lucinie also stayed behind, and on her knees, after the others left, but it had never occurred to Sister Jeanne to censure her for this. Nevertheless, she could not deny to herself that this was how she felt. Sister Lucinie's attitude was qualitatively different from that of Sister St. Jean. It was impossible to doubt the sincerity. As for the other, Sister Jeanne could not decide to what extent she was sincere. It was possible that her urge to show off did not go so deep as to corrupt the nature of her actions, that this need to make a display of her religion came only from her sense of security in her faith, and from a natural simplicity absent in the other nuns. Sister Jeanne recognized, nevertheless, that this analysis was inadequate. Security in her faith, perhaps, but not natural simplicity. That was something nobody could attribute to Sister St. Jean. She never had the slightest doubt about the correctness of her views. She was unyielding in her judgment and severe in her criticism, and these characteristics combined with a fixed and suspicious distrust to exclude all thought of candor.

Probably Sister St. Jean's distrust had aroused a mutual reaction in Sister Jeanne. The young nun felt that this was at the very base of her dislike. The old lady's excessive severity and her total inability to forgive or to adopt a favorable interpretation where a doubt existed raised a barrier between them. She even thought that she discerned in Sister St. Jean's speech a generalization of this error, unintended, perhaps, but nevertheless revealing the extent to which a wrong attitude had gained possession of her soul.

Sister Jeanne did not define these conclusions in so many words. Lacking factual evidence for many of them, she was falling back once more on her intuition. The

only points she could definitely blame Sister St. Jean
for were her severity and her love of showing off. Nothing else could be deduced directly from her speech or
her actions. She put man in a humiliating position, face
to face with his tragic destiny, and deprived of outside
help. But she was logical. She accepted this position for
herself and the distressingly bitter conclusion she drew did
not invalidate her stand. Sister St. Jean was not really
guilty of a fault meriting either punishment or Sister
Jeanne's suspicions.

Apart from all this, the young woman did not think
that her analysis explained Sister Dominique's displeasure, nor did she want to explain it. Sister St. Jean's age,
it seemed to her, was of itself enough to save her from
every danger, as well as from every grave sin. The final
conclusion to which all her reflections accordingly led
was merely to accuse herself. First of all, even though
she had been very careful not to formulate such a judgment, she considered herself guilty of rash judgment in
suspecting her companion, since she had been unable to
provide any solid basis for the charge of unkindness which
had formulated itself of its own accord against her. She
asked pardon for this wrong and promised to continue
to pray until midnight and to fast the following day as a
punishment. After this she finally came to a reasonable
conclusion, deciding that something she herself had done
had called for the Mother Superior's correction. She began, accordingly, to examine her own conscience again.

She naturally found there certain things with which
she could reproach herself, such as having experienced
inner feelings of impatience with the complaints of her
patient that morning, not to mention the more recent

uncalled-for severity toward Sister St. Jean. But Sister Dominique could not have intended to punish her for these things, knowing nothing about them. Perhaps then her Superior's annoyance had resulted from Sister Jeanne's getting home somewhat late that evening. It was a quarter to seven when she reached the house, because her patient had had a bad turn and wanted her to stay. The Mother Superior was strict on matters of discipline, but she knew she was quick to pardon such digressions when the sister's duty made them unavoidable, and even if she had a criticism to make, she was accustomed to make it in private.

And that left Sister Jeanne with no theory except perhaps that the heat had tired out Sister Dominique to the point of getting the better of her customary gentleness and goodness and making her decide for once to act, if not in a wholly unjust way, at least with undue severity. And so Sister Jeanne told herself that this punishment, which in any case was deserved for other reasons, had been good for her. It had led her to study her behavior and make a salutary examination of conscience, and finally had forced her to clarify her thinking on the subject of judging the actions of others, a thing she had been avoiding. Yet not even this analysis sufficed to clear up all her problems. Sister Jeanne now saw that it involved a criticism of Sister Dominique which was not only uncharitable but lacking in the respect due the Superior. The best thing, she decided, was to ask her forgiveness tomorrow. As for now, the solution was to make her peace with God by accepting His will with love. She closed her eyes. Joy welled up in her heart and carried her toward Jesus.

Chapter VI

INTUITION rather than eyesight told Sister Anne of the Cross that the tall, slim figure was Sister Lucinie. Night was coming fast, and the gloom made it possible to confuse, for example, Sister Jeanne and Sister Pélagie. Both of them were slim like Sister Lucinie but nevertheless she wasn't like any of the others. She wore the heavy medieval black woollen habit like a ceremonial costume. Her way of walking, in spite of the strict discipline of the novitiate, retained a distinctive charm, and her unhurried and formal gestures revealed a dignity royal in their simplicity. Actually, they were not nearly so deliberate as they seemed. It was rather the precision of movement, the economy of performance, and the definite relation to a certain end that conveyed this impression.

40

A further characteristic was that they never occurred without a reason, and nevertheless these slender hands were capable of performing a great deal of work in a very short time.

"Reverend Mother is upset," Sister Lucinie said, bending close to Sister Anne of the Cross. "Because of the late hour, she feared an accident."

Sister Lucinie could never speak low. Always she used the same full, warm tones, so clear that her words could be understood at a distance. This at times annoyed the listener, and the Novice Mistress had tried unsuccessfully to make her adopt a lower tone. Sister Anne of the Cross often teased her, pretending that she could overhear Sister Lucinie's confessions, and predicting that she would spend at least five thousand years in purgatory. This evening in particular, in a public place, the voice shocked her because it sounded almost like a rebuke.

"I stayed longer than usual," she answered quickly, "because my patient died."

Then she fell silent, her annoyance calmed by the touch of a cool hand on hers. Sister Anne never regretted having become a nun, accepting all the joys and all the sorrows, among them the fact that she would never have children. Nor did she waste her time thinking about this disappointment, which simply lay deep and unformulated below the level of consciousness, checking even the impulse to play with babies. Besides, though she loved their charm, children did not really interest her too much. What she sought was rather a spiritual relationship, a friendship based on the mind, brightened by and directed toward God. For the first time in her life

41

she believed that she had found this in Sister Lucinie, and she loved the young nun with not just the same warm friendship she entertained for the old Mother Superior or her other companions, but with motherly and watchful concern. However, a silent sense of discretion hid this from the others, and it seemed even from the young woman herself, for she responded only with restraint, giving no indication other than a smile.

Previously Sister Lucinie had enjoyed a superabundance of happiness which she spread equally all around, and this explosive joy had given the impression of sentimental extravagance and lack of reserve. In reality, however, she had revealed nothing of her inmost thoughts or affections, or of the source of her joy. This joy she had expressed in songs, laughter, and dances, those unhappy dances Sister St. Jean had called shameful, and by throwing herself wholeheartedly into her work. But what were the thoughts and inner feelings urging her to such actions? That secret was never revealed to anyone.

Sister Lucinie lived in the open, addressing whatever she had to say equally to all, but keeping her spiritual life completely closed to outside influences. Sister Anne of the Cross thought she could occasionally discern a special attention paid to herself, the gift of a holy picture, some small annoying task performed for her, certain smiling glances that seemed to share and approve her mood. But there was no clear guarantee that an equal affection corresponded to her love, especially since the sudden and gloomy development of Sister Lucinie's character.

Sister Anne of the Cross, like all the members of the community, was disturbed by the change, but nobody succeeded in piercing the young woman's reserve, and she did not dare formulate questions that Sister Lucinie's attitude indicated would be unwelcome. Nevertheless, the gesture this evening, this consoling hand resting on hers, these fingers which grasped her own and retained their grip while the two nuns continued on their way, finally gave her the truth for which she had waited so long, and Sister Anne of the Cross in turn tightened her own grasp in an outburst of affection.

"I am so pleased that Reverend Mother picked you to come to meet me," she explained. "To walk back with you in the dusk, to share the beauty of this wonderful evening, to comfort you in your distress — I could feel it from a distance — all this is a blessing for me."

They walked the entire length of the public park, their black figures wrapped in the shadow of the trees. They could make out vaguely against the hazy pallor of their linen guimpes and cornettes what their faces looked like at night. The perfume of the last flowering magnolias and lilacs floated over the two silent women. Sister Lucinie was thinking that the scent of the trees served as a means of expression and permitted a form of communication between the plants and man. The gratuitousness of the gift, accepted and not seized like a plucked flower or a garnered ear of wheat, made the understanding between the two all the more precious, and though Sister Lucinie no more understood this language than she did that of the animals, she felt that it revealed a thought, a secret to be guessed, a soul related in its qualities to her own.

On reaching the first houses, the nuns relaxed their grip, hiding their hands in the sleeves of their habits.

43

But they remained close together as they continued home-ward, their minds alert, each waiting for the other to speak. They were close to the house when Sister Lucinie did so.

"I have been wanting to ask your advice, but did not dare, and now it's late."

The changed voice filled Sister Anne with concern. Trembling, she stopped and studied her young companion's face, holding the door half open as she looked. She could make out only the piercing eyes shining from an oval face almost hidden in the darkness. But the disturbed tones revealed better than could any expression Sister Lucinie's need for help.

"Let me mention it to Reverend Mother. I'm sure she'd approve of our having another private chat."

"I just don't know," the young woman said in a whisper. "What I wanted to ask you is quite unimportant, and besides she has problems enough already. I'd rather nobody else knew about it, but do whatever you think best."

"I'll ask Reverend Mother," Sister Anne of the Cross answered gently. "It's the best thing to do."

"You really think so?"

The older nun would never forget for her entire life the frightened look in the eyes revealed by the light of the corridor and the agitation expressed in the question. Sister Lucinie seemed suddenly to be a bird caught in a snare. Her hands lost their habitual control and raised themselves in what seemed a gesture of self-protection against an invisible fate.

Chapter VII

"A T L A S T we can talk," said Sister Anne of the Cross.

The door to the corridor had just closed behind the Mother Superior, and the two nuns were again alone. The midmorning heat was beginning to find its way into the room, and a beam of light pierced a hole in the shutter to shine diagonally across the room between the two women and rest on a pile of handkerchiefs that grew as Sister Lucinie worked.

Not seeming to hear her companion's invitation, she now spread a napkin on the ironing board. She pushed the shining iron back and forth with deft hands, and she followed the movement with her eyes, ashamed of herself for the initiative she had taken the other evening. For three days she had anticipated this interview with distress and confusion. At times it seemed to her that her problem was not nearly so important as she had suggested and would merely provoke the jests of her old friend. At other times, on the contrary, she feared that perhaps she was underestimating the significance of this spiritual conflict. She had hesitated a long time before giving the hint she had given the other evening, and she had not expected Sister Anne of the Cross to bring the matter so quickly to Sister Dominique's attention. She had wanted very badly to avoid this happening, not for fear of anything the Mother Superior might do to her, but rather to spare her an additional problem. Now, she realized, she could no longer avoid telling her also the difficulties she was experiencing, both because Sister Anne of the Cross would insist, and because she did not want to suggest that she lacked confidence in Sister Dominique.

"You wanted to say?" Sister Anne of the Cross was determined not to lose her chance.

Sister Lucinie, still silent, studied the gnarled finger joints of her companion and the scarcely perceptible movement of the thumb counting the rosary beads. She waited while Sister Anne recited two more Hail Marys, joining mentally in the prayer.

"I was saying" — she blushed as she repeated the phrase, and tried to ease the tension by maneuvering the iron to press with more than usual care the embroideries of the altar cloth — "I am not sure that I believe in God, or rather that I believe in God in the way the Catholic faith proposes for our belief."

A long silence followed. To Sister Lucinie's relief, it was not broken by the rebukes or exclamations of astonishment she had anticipated from Sister Anne of the Cross. The dust continued its silly dance in the beam of light, three more beads slipped through the praying fingers, and the iron crushed down the scalloped festoons and grains of wheat embroidered on the altar linen.

"Have you spoken about this to your confessor?"

"Yes," Sister Lucinie answered. "At least I have told him that God no longer answers my call. He has talked to me of periods of dryness and the need for spiritual reading and prayers. But if you forgive my saying so, I have been aware of all that for a long time and for a long time I have been praying and reading, and still I always continue in my doubt just like the first day. I fulfill all my duties here with little effort and to the best of my ability because I love them, because I enjoy the life in this house, and because my sense of right is not shaken even though it is detached from God. I think that our work is still a good one. Only . . . "

The young nun folded the starched cloth carefully, running her fingers lightly and lovingly over the raised decorations and the cross in the center. She laid it on the mantelpiece, then hesitated for a moment before choosing another piece of linen. She did not know what to say next, and the tears that she could no longer hold back welled from her eyes and rolled down her cheeks one by one. Sister Anne looked out the window, praying more rapidly than before, and all her Hail Marys formed a vibrant backdrop adorned with her single passionate appeal: "My God, show me how to help her."

"The one thing that tormented me," Sister Lucinie continued, "was the question of devotion, the correct religious attitude. What I mean is that my attitude had

47

ceased to be other than a pretence, though not entirely a hypocrisy, you understand. I continued my devotions as one takes medicine, either to prove the reality of my indifference or to cure myself. I thought that if God existed in spite of my denial, He would come to help me. I did it through loyalty to an outdated image. But now, getting no answer, I think it may be better to give up the effort and stop appearing in your eyes as something I no longer am."

"This change dates from your quarrel with Sister St. Jean?"

"No. Sister St. Jean did not cause it. Her rebuke at best crystallized the former vague impressions. I was living in a circle of happiness. The work was so easy, the house peaceable, companions who treated me with gentle indulgence, a poverty that caused no deprivation, detachment from everything here below, and a sense of following the true road with joy and exactness. You understand, if a temptation arose, I had only to think of God and everything cleared itself. This light would well up inside me in an explosion of joy. But for some time I had begun to have doubts about myself, just about myself. I would think that I must certainly be deceived, that one could not traverse this stony road or pass through this narrow gate so easily, that I had found no thorns, and that my joy was perhaps a defect. I did not often dwell on these ideas, and, in any case, they did not present themselves in specific terms but rather as an unpleasant background.

"Then we came to that miserable day of the Epiphany. Sister St. Jean's rebukes fitted exactly into my doubts. That evening and the few days that followed I tried to decide on one of two alternatives, either to accept joyfully a humble and easy life, or to adopt the glum and serious attitude that Sister St. Jean recommended.

"Before that time you could hear me laugh even in the chapel. You I loved in particular, because you always saw the comic side of things. I loved Sister Perpétue, too, for she also would join in my laughter, though I must confess it occasionally fell a trifle short of due respect for divine things. Of course I never mocked them, but I treated Jesus as a companion rather than as God. I gossiped with Him at all hours of the day, included Him in the jokes I played on the nuns, complained to Him, told Him what to do.

"All at once I realized I had been wrong. Of course Sister St. Jean's criticisms also shared responsibility for my sadness. I reached a point where I could no longer shake them off. Each time they came back with the same tremendous force and crushed my resistance. I appealed to God, but there was no answer, and I remained alone in the depths of my misery. I then decided that my duty was to accept the criticisms and humble myself under their weight. Jesus no longer helped me. From that time I was alone. Now you must realize that my faith was not the result of a chain of logical analysis, but that it came from a personal experience. I believed in God because I felt Him. Now all that collapsed, and I realized, in looking for proofs, that nothing proves for me that God exists."

A silence followed. Ordinarily Sister Anne of the Cross did not need much time to prepare an answer, but today her thoughts clarified themselves more slowly and she needed intervals of silent reflection which Sister Lucinie found almost unendurable. All the ideas the young woman had just expressed now seemed to her false, and she suspected an inconsistency in her complaints. The problem, as she saw it, was that she was making too precise a division in her faith. The reality was more subtle, so that her words exaggerated and distorted her thought. Her panic at the idea of confiding in Mother Superior, as Sister Anne of the Cross had insisted, her fear of not being able to express more than an unsubstantial and vague feeling, had led her to present conclusions that were far from exact. She believed that her difficulty in explaining her emotions would produce in the older nun the same lack of understanding that had occurred with her confessor. She recalled, with one of those quick flushes of color that made her so childish and charming, the feeling of solitude and abandon, the bitter reaction tinged with annoyance which the priest's lack of concern had produced. For her the problem had become tragic, but the others did not seem to appreciate the depth of her suffering or recognize its true value.

The others, she thought. First the confessor and now Sister Anne of the Cross. Sister Lucinie found herself caught in a web of pressing circumstances, and the more she thought about the apparent lack of understanding of the old priest, the more it worried her and warped her relations with him. She had later confessed this fault, including it in a general accusation without specifying who was the object of her judgment. The priest had paid no attention. He never asked questions, listening in silence and at the end specifying some prayers or spiritual reading as a penance. As a result, the confessions gradually took on a passive character, quite different from what they had been in the motherhouse.

There, the spiritual director had discussed each fault, placing it under the microscope to reduce it to its proper insignificance, yet to make it at the same time absolutely intolerable. Relations between him and his penitents were, in consequence, invested with an atmosphere of fear mixed with extreme confidence. Without perhaps attaining the sanctity which his flock generously attributed to him, he represented a safe way, an efficacious help in reaching God.

Here, the knowledge of the priest's indifference did not produce this fear of God nor the emotional consolation that had passed from the former confessor to his penitents. Instead, a different kind of uneasiness existed. The distraction of the priest was pretended. He remembered every admission and did not hesitate from time to time to make ambiguous allusions which filled the guilty ones with confusion and caused much amusement to the old priest. No doubt these innuendoes lacked severity or evil intent. He only meant to tease them, but Sister Lucinie did not appreciate that kind of fun.

Confession was for her one of the principal difficulties of religion. She found admissions of guilt extremely painful, and had once said so to the former confessor.

"I believe," he answered, "that you think too much about yourself. You should forget yourself so completely that you cease to imagine that your state of mind concerns others. The low opinion a confessor might form of you can only bring you further along the road of humility you have chosen.

"Introspection and concern about their salvation often cause devout people to develop a sense of self-importance, to overestimate their virtues and defects. All these things

51

have value only in relation to God and to society. In themselves they mean nothing.

"Then what difference does it make what opinion a priest has of you, if you are of little importance and indeed scarcely capable of being described as existing on your own account, especially as this priest is of no more worth than you and you have an absolute guarantee that he cannot communicate his opinion to anyone else? You might almost call him a part of your own conscience. He exists only because of your intelligent choice, just as your mathematical knowledge does.

"Be a little more humble. Do not distort your confessor's personality. In the confessional let him be a freely chosen judge, and outside merely a voice, a reflection, a soul, but not a man."

She recalled this lesson, but she found herself unable to apply it in the present case. Nevertheless, a useful phrase recurred in her memory: "You should forget yourself to such an extent as not to think that the state of your soul torments anyone else." That she had not forgotten. Her current problem revolved around God but in relation to her own soul. She tried to make up her mind about the reality or unreality of God in order to establish the moral meaning of her new spiritual attitude. Another phrase used by her confessor in the motherhouse came to mind: "The person is important only in relation to God or to society." Sister Lucinie should have studied this suggestion more deeply but she had never taken very long to think about it nor had she ever discussed it with others, at least in the past. She accepted the statement without drawing a concrete conclusion. She preferred to take her stand on the life of

Christ, reliving it in her imagination. She discussed it mentally, going over the details again and again, describing to herself the physical characteristics of appearance and of scene, until at times, though very infrequently, a brief fleeting vision called forth her full concentration and made her ready to recapture with all the concentrated force of her emotions the image that had forever disappeared.

This practice she loved dearly, yet it did not achieve contact with God. Rather did He flee, the moment she tried to reach Him, though at other times He approached her of His own accord and entered her soul unexpectedly. He did not give her a clear knowledge, but He flooded her awareness with a vague and sweet joy so that she knew that He was present. How did she know that? Who gave her such an assurance? In fact, she had no such assurance, but its absence did not change her belief. And now for some considerable time this sense of union had left her or at least had suffered a qualitative change, becoming less certain and lacking sweetness.

Sister Lucinie again addressed her companion. "I don't know whether or not I believe in God. It seems to me that a strange force lives in the center of my soul, close to where my heart is. I cannot call this force God and I do not know in an intellectual, logical, or experimental way what it is. But, even if I do not participate in its life, even if it seems inactive within me, it pushes me outside myself, places me at the outer edge of my personality, at what I might call the limit of my skin. At times I even go outside to take a look at myself. I see not my physical person but this interior and strange force, like a bewildering night, a terrifying unknown, this

53

force that I could almost deny but the absolute truth of which I sense, and which I intuitively believe to be God."

"But if that is so, daughter, you believe in God."

Was it this assurance or this affectionate word that Sister Lucinie was looking for? Probably both. And yet she needed no assurance for what she understood obscurely within herself. The explanation that she had just presented in as clear a manner as she was able had enlightened her as to the true meaning of her suffering and of her disclosures. The purpose of these latter was to create a bond of affection, to arouse the mother instinct. The hidden, indefinable threat that she had endured for months was stressing the childish aspects of her character. She drew nearer Sister Anne of the Cross because she felt that this nun was ready to make the sacrifices of a mother for her. She knew that she was strong, she loved her, and she felt herself at the end of her strength. Only her timidity and her fear that she had misinterpreted the true feelings of the old nun had kept her from asking help sooner. At this precise moment, when the word for which she had waited so long finally let its healing balm drop on her soul, she suddenly wanted to throw aside the stiff white collar and fall on her knees, laying her head in her companion's lap and closing her eyes under the gentle touch of the toil-hardened fingers. But she continued her task of starching the linen.

"You see," Sister Anne of the Cross said, "Jesus has accepted you as His spouse just like thousands and thousands of other women all over the globe. He has, in fact, quite a harem."

54

"Oh," Sister Lucinie exclaimed, shocked and amused. "What a way to speak of Him!"

"The difference is that, unlike you, I am no longer in the last days of my honeymoon. I have known Him all my life and I respect Him, as you do, but I can tell Him truths you would never dare breathe."

A gleam of malice sparkled through the screen of wrinkles surrounding the old nun's eyes. Sister Lucinie looked at her, unbelieving, her lips half open, neither daring to hold back the irresistible smile provoked by her companion's face nor yet to yield to the humor that seemed to her hardly reverent. Such a way of expressing the relations between the old lady and Jesus indicated an outlook so strictly matrimonial that she did not dare accept it.

"Yes," Sister Anne of the Cross assured her, reading her thoughts. "He is our spouse. The marriage is a mystic one, but nonetheless a marriage, and I am in an excellent position to see for myself after these many years of service that it has at least one defect."

"Sister," Sister Lucinie interrupted impetuously, "what are you saying?"

"You see," the other continued calmly, "you still believe in Him and you love Him, because my words hurt you so deeply. Nevertheless, I don't take them back, and if I am wrong, He will react like those old couples who sulk and quarrel all day long but who cannot go out for a walk unless both go together. He will forgive me. My complaint, then, is that He is fickle."

Sister Lucinie's laugh rang out gaily, that high-pitched laugh, rising and falling tunefully, which the community had forgotten and which sounded to the old nun as welcome as the bells at Easter.

"You can't deny it," Sister Anne of the Cross said dolefully, pretending an annoyance which her dancing eyes denied. "He tires of us one after the other, looks for new favorites, takes us back, abandons us again. He wants us to want Him. He comes only on a day we forget Him or when the heart goes adrift — as yours is doing — and loses Him."

"No," Sister Lucinie said in a low voice, "not that."

Sister Anne of the Cross fell silent. Sister Lucinie took up the iron and began again to move it back and forward, but it was clear that her heart was not in her work and that she was once more growing weak inside. Her laughter had signified no more than a momentary clearing in a sky covered with storm clouds.

"It's not quite that easy," the young woman said finally. "I believe and I doubt. I no longer know where I stand. I need a proof, some logical argument."

"God is not logic," Sister Anne interrupted. "I tell you that He has His defects. He does not adapt Himself to our whims."

She smiled at the failure of her little joke.

"I cannot continue to honor a possibly fictitious person or thing. I must find out if I am speaking to God or to nothingness," Sister Lucinie said.

"But weren't you telling me a moment ago that you felt God within you?"

"No, I feel a power within me. I believe that this power is God, but I am not sure. You realize that I am capable of entertaining an illusion, that my body can deceive me. I know that I believe in God, that all the depths of my being submit to Him, that even if reason proved to me that He did not exist I should still go on believing in Him. Nevertheless, I need a proof, a rational conviction."

"Why do you need this rational conviction, as you call it, if your experience already tells you all you want to know?"

"My experience is incomplete," Sister Lucinie insisted with an expression of annoyance. "Nothing emerges clearly in all of this."

"That's enough. I am going to tell you what I think. You are an ungrateful wretch."

Sister Anne of the Cross stood up angrily and lifted her hands so that for a moment Sister Lucinie was sure she was going to strike her. Instead, she merely placed her hard fingertips on her companion's arms and drew them close to her.

"You have no right to refuse to believe in the presence of such a mark of favor. I believe in God humbly, every day since I was a child. I was not good, but for Him I have become good. I have entreated Him to come to me, but He has kept me in the emotional aridity of our convent. You know what I am trying to say. On every side, no matter where you look, every face wears a smile, every hand is stretched out in a friendly way, every prayer is purified and lifted up on the prayers of others, every task becomes more important because it has been offered to heaven. But behind all of that nothing is revealed in an identifiable shape. Behind the humanity of the act, the humanity of the walls is ranged, and behind that again the humanity of the world, and meanwhile God, for whom all this is done, refuses to approve or even notice. To continue alone for sixty years along the ordinary road, to fumble in the darkness in order to reach the light on the other side of death, and to do that without ever once entertaining a doubt against faith, in spite of the doubts of body and spirit, while you see yourself elected, the recipient of this grace, of this magnificence, and you refuse it! I feel like crushing you against the wall, if only I had not so much respect for Our Lord."

"Sister Anne," Sister Lucinie said in a low voice, "you are hurting me, and I am burning the linen."

The old nun's excitement wore itself out slowly. She released her prisoner and plucked the electric cord from the socket. Sister Lucinie wept as she continued to press a stiff and shining cornette which she held with her left hand.

"Take a moment's rest," Sister Anne of the Cross told her.

Sister Lucinie obeyed, placing the hot iron on a stand and collecting carefully about her the pieces that needed mending. She started on the job right away, gritting her teeth to hold back her tears. Nevertheless, they forced themselves one by one out of the corners of her eyes, and she wiped them off with dainty movements of her finger.

"Why don't you let yourself go and have a good cry?" Sister Anne of the Cross asked.

She loved that nimble forefinger, that unwillingness to allow the eyelids to redden, that effort to hide suffering. A readiness to display one's grief was a defect common to the entire little community. Without going to the extreme of Sister St. Jean, who waved her tears like a flag, most of the nuns were happy to let them be seen.

Sister Anne of the Cross, like Sister Dominique, had just about reached the age where her tear ducts were pretty well dried up, but nevertheless she still on rare occasions found herself in a situation in which the sad pleasure of tears calmed her. She did not show them off ostentatiously, but neither did she hide them. She admired Sister Lucinie's correctness. Basically, of course, it came neither from the discipline of the convent, the virtue of joy, nor the detachment taught in the novitiate, but from her previous education. For Sister Lucinie, it would have been an evidence of vulgarity, a lack of all dignity, to make a public issue of any intimate emotion, most of all an unpleasant one. She kept this stamp, and without being pained by the contrary conduct of her companions, she found herself unable to imitate them. Previously her gaiety had provided a point of contact, but since the Epiphany, when this link was broken, she had lived spiritually alone. Her distress and humility had made her whisper her problems to Sister Anne of the Cross, for she no longer judged herself capable of making a correct choice between different aims and lines of conduct. She already regretted that decision, notwithstanding the tenderness of the older woman and the faith that had breathed new courage into her.

Nevertheless, her companion's most recent suggestion produced the very opposite effect of that intended. Sister Lucinie dried her eyes and turned her back to Sister Anne of the Cross, fearing to betray her weakness again. To distract herself, she tried to follow the movements on the street through the slits in the closed shutters.

"And if," she asked in a slightly hoarse voice, "if this force was not God, but . . ." she hesitated, tapping out her tension through her fingertips on the windowpane, and added abruptly, "the devil?"

The question made Sister Anne of the Cross grow taut. She took a long look at the slightly bowed back. All she could see was a tall, dark outline. The black veil of her headdress hid the vivid whiteness of her collar and her cornette as well as the slight figure and the pale bloodless hand tapping on the glass. The old nun felt that she was looking at a flower seen in a deep shadow but still transparent and able to stir the senses, although now lacking all material reality of form and touch.

Sister Lucinie went on in a broken voice.

"Do you not think that only a tremendous pride would make me believe in God's presence within me? This power I experience remains nameless. Though I feel it, it does not reveal its identity. Should I not lack all true humility were I to draw such a conclusion?"

The depth of her feeling finally broke down her verbal reserve.

"I tell you I am not trying to flatter myself, I simply register a fact. I am not proud. I know that I am not good, I know that I do not merit such a grace, and that I do not have the strength to bear it. Because of my humility I experience these doubts and I am afraid that my doubts may be sinful. Do you remember the Sermon on the Mount — that the sin against the Spirit is the hardest to forgive? Must I be tempted by God alone?"

"But this power," Sister Anne of the Cross insisted gently, "does this power drive you to wrongdoing, does it raise evil thoughts within you? I mean, other than the doubt we are talking about?"

"No," Sister Lucinie answered. "To be quite exact,

there is no question of it speaking. It is simply there. When I experience it, I become absorbed in it. I have no desire to do evil."

"Do you recall," her companion asked, "the scene described in the Gospel, where the Pharisees accused Christ of healing with the help of the prince of demons?"

"Yes. He had just healed a blind man and it was a very hot day."

The old woman's surprise showed on her face as she looked at her companion. She did not recall that St. Matthew had mentioned this detail and she suspected that it reflected rather an interior light on the scene than an exact recollection of the biblical text.

"Do you remember Christ's answer?"

"Yes." Sister Lucinie smiled and recited: " 'And Jesus, knowing their thoughts, said to them: Every kingdom divided against itself shall be made desolate. . . . If Satan cast out Satan, he is divided against himself: how then shall his kingdom stand?' "

She left her place by the wall and laid a hand mechanically on the iron.

"I want to thank you. I have never reflected enough on what the gospel teaches us. It cannot be the devil. But what if, nevertheless, I were deceiving myself? If I were merely in the presence of a projection of my own mind? I could be going crazy."

"No," Sister Anne of the Cross protested, moving over to sit in Sister Dominique's favorite chair. "If you were losing your mind, we would have all kinds of details by which to recognize this fact. I believe that it is your duty to submit yourself to this force, and when I give this advice, I steer you toward what is folly in the worldly sense of the word, but we do not take our vows in order to guarantee ourselves a quiet existence. We come to God and we must follow Him on every road, even on what seems an unreasonable one. In my opinion, certain types of foolishness lead to such a degree of purity that the prize is worth all the sufferings involved in attaining it. To believe in a course that leads toward God, to raise oneself up by means of a tremendous effort of love toward the form which He assumes, this is surely to go toward Him."

"I do not believe that there is here a question of love."

Sister Anne of the Cross, again astonished, studied Sister Lucinie. She could not envisage the possibility of thinking about God without loving Him. She saw Him only under one very clear aspect, that of the Son, and this opened such a deep gulf between her concept and that of her companion that she did not think she should try to bridge it, for it was something she knew nothing about. Sister Lucinie loved the Son, perhaps not in precisely the same terms as her older companion, but with equal sincerity. Nevertheless, the Trinity, and particularly the unity of the Trinity, remained uppermost in her mind, and she was never able to separate entirely the Father and the Holy Ghost from this human aspect. The meekness of the Word was something grafted onto the universal power of God.

"I am afraid," the young woman confessed.

Chapter VIII

T H E   R O O M slept in the half-light of drawn curtains and closed shutters. A very old woman lay under the lace-edged sheet; her eyes were haggard, her mouth gaping, her wrists twisted.

Sister Pélagie, seated unseen at a distance from the bed, said her rosary and watched the sick woman. The prayer ground itself out mechanically, providing no relief for her tedium. Outside, the hot wind from the Libyan desert blew in long, howling gusts, and the nun dreamed of her convent, of the white cell, of the bed where she longed to stretch herself, one arm over her eyes, and abandon herself comfortably to her dreams. Here, she had to suffer and anticipate the whims of a woman who enjoyed hurting her, to listen to the meaningless exclamations, to endure her own weariness while trying to hide in the background because even her presence irritated the sick woman's nerves. It did not annoy her to give in to her patient's whims. Indeed, she sympathized with the old lady whose moods were conditioned by the neglect of all her children, and she blamed them for not being able to sacrifice their own convenience and accept this long and painful sickness as a duty. But she kept her opinion to herself. Perhaps she might have been able to be a little more cheerful in her conversation, to smile a little more often, as the sick woman's daughter had suggested. But she no longer found the strength to do more than her strict duty. Those days were gone. Now, she was satisfied if she did merely what she had to.

No doubt this unwillingness to become involved was born of fatigue, but it also had deep roots in her mental condition, in her vague dissatisfaction with herself and her whole life. This moral decay had a definite cause and all that Sister Pélagie needed was a little will power to put a stop to it, but she loved her extended escapes to dreamland and the opportunity they provided to forget completely her ordinary life.

God was withdrawing from her. The previous month He was still fighting, annoying her when her thoughts wandered, appearing in the middle of the silly episodes in which her imagination delighted. But her dream had slowly overcome the opposition and taken the upper hand so that it prevented her from reading to the end of the page, danced among the threads of her sewing, slipped between the folds of a surgical dressing, made all prayer impossible, interrupted her conversations. She dawdled in it, no longer concerned with the consequences, reassured by a certain purity of the content of her thoughts. She never experienced sensual pleasure from her dreams, at least not as she understood the term. Her dreams of love were confined to mental pictures of the ballroom, the exchange of light talk, flowers, and greetings. It was a kind of courtship, but inconsistent, in that it always broke down before marriage, then skipped over to resume as a matter of course between two disembodied persons whose relations prospered and expanded in a fanciful and impossible atmosphere.

All this insipidity was gaining control of her, crushing her by the lack of consistency of its outlines and by the fluttering ideas impossible to formulate precisely. It was separating her from her companions and the sick people in her charge and even from her actions which she carried out mechanically. She was reaching a point where she could read aloud for a long time without understanding a single word she said, where she ate a meal without distinguishing the dishes placed before her. Her thoughts held her at a distance from herself, thoughts that were forever changing and being renewed, always concerned with one general theme subject to only minor variations. All this approached a kind of sleepwalking where everything lost its reality, so that gradually she found more satisfaction in this semiconscious state than in the dream itself.

The wind rattled the shutters, and the sick woman whimpered. Sister Pélagie changed the ice packs on her forehead and switched on the fan. Then she noticed a change in the woman's condition. The dilated eyes had ceased to protest, the lips were silent, and the breath grew weaker. She started running toward the door, then

65

changed her mind and rang the bell. Nobody answered. She rang again, then returned to the dying woman. The mouth was closed, the breathing scarcely perceptible. Big tears rolled down the stiffening jaws.

"Can you hear me?" Sister Pélagie whispered, laying her fingers on those of the dying woman. "Shall I call a priest?"

She looked hard into the eyes that no longer moved but could still see her.

"Can I leave you for a minute to telephone the doctor?"

Suddenly she panicked, overcome by the silence and by the indifference of the house. She rushed over, pressed the bell push for an entire minute, then came back to the bed. The panic passed, and again she became calm when she took the paralyzed fingers into her hands. Death came quietly, softly. Three short breaths carried with them the sorrows of a lifetime and restored the nun's tranquillity. She joined the hands now forever still on the emaciated chest, pressed the eyelids which half closed in response, and left the room.

There was no sign of life anywhere in the house. She checked the empty kitchen, explored the entire ground floor, and then went upstairs. Not knowing the ins and outs, she began to knock at each door, a sensation of fear combined with anger mounting steadily inside her. Finally, fearing that someone might surprise her in such a place and suspect her of lack of discretion, she stopped her search on hearing a smothered laugh in one of the rooms. There was no answer to her knock on the door. Nevertheless, she knew somebody was there and she quickly opened and closed the door. Then she waited.

66

Almost immediately a young woman put her head out challengingly, but she immediately changed her attitude and forced a smile, pulling the door shut with one hand and with the other straightening out the front of her dressing gown and her dishevelled hair.

"You need something, Sister?" she asked coldly.

The tone annoyed Sister Pélagie.

"I have been calling for nearly an hour," she said, astonished at the hate and threat her voice conveyed. "Your grandmother is dead."

"That's impossible," the young woman protested, doubly frightened by this unexpected death and by the fear the nun had aroused. "What could I do? I am alone."

A chair scraped in the room.

"I find that hard to believe," Sister Pélagie commented tartly. "You must come down and help me dress the corpse before it stiffens."

"No, no," the young woman protested urgently. "I couldn't even look."

The nun eyed her more sympathetically. She was little more than a girl. Her lips were coated thick with lipstick, her hair was dyed, her nails shone with a blood-red polish. The fear was real, but it also contained an external element. Her major concern was that if she left the room, she might fail to arrange another meeting with its temporary occupant or even explain to him this stupid and ill-timed interruption. That factor weighed more heavily with her than her reluctance to contemplate death. An awkward moment, indeed. The two women could hear the irritated footsteps pacing back and forth, the efforts to avoid making noise which failed to hide the creaking of shoes, the fall of a book, the scraping of a chair.

Her anger left Sister Pélagie almost immediately. Having found somebody, she was no longer wandering around blindly, and that was enough for her. Besides, she refused to condemn, for she knew nothing about this rather vulgar young woman, and she never sought to inflict pain. Pity seized her in the presence of the concern written on the painted face.

"Don't be afraid," she said gently. "Death is nothing. I'll go on back down. You can call the convent and have someone come to help me. Then, if you give me what I need, I'm sure I can make the final preparations by myself. Take a few minutes to calm down before you join me."

She turned away with a light step. What she had done was perhaps not quite proper, but a great joy took possession of her because she had succeeded in controlling her anger and comforting one in grief. Jesus had said: "He who is without sin, let him cast the first stone." She had almost cast that first stone, but her hand had fallen before she had actually done so. She knew that what the young woman was doing was harmful to society and to herself, but it was not her job either to reprimand or to accuse. Her duty as a nun was to give the gift of herself by helping others.

Passing the telephone, she called the convent and was relieved to be instantly assured that Sister Lucinie would join her as quickly as possible. She undressed the dead woman, listening to the noise outside, fearing that her companion might be kept waiting at the door because there was no servant around to open it. But while

68

she was preparing cotton wool and a piece of cloth to tie up the lower jaw that hung down distressingly, Sister Lucinie, silent as always, appeared beside her.

"What a fright you gave me," Sister Pélagie whispered. "How did you get in?"

She looked with amazement at the newcomer. It was indeed Sister Lucinie but something indefinable had changed her subtly. Sister Pélagie could not even decide just what the change was. Perhaps the light in the room affected the color of her face, for she held herself the same as always — very erect figure, hands in sleeves of habit, forehead high.

"An officer was leaving just as I arrived and he showed me where to come. What can I do to help?"

"Nothing just yet. This is the home of the sleeping beauty, beyond a doubt. Not a soul around. Or at least nobody who can help. I telephoned for the priest and I don't know what more can be done."

The door opened and the dead woman's granddaughter came in. Sister Pélagie noted with surprise that in fifteen minutes she had completely removed her make-up, even cleaning the red varnish off her nails. Not a strand of hair was out of place, and end curls were tucked demurely under an invisible hairnet. Instead of the long silk dressing gown, she now wore a little dark dress that made her look even younger.

"I brought this," she said in a low voice, handing Sister Pélagie some sheets and a black dress belonging to the dead woman. "Her linen is over there in that chest."

She stationed herself at the foot of the bed and began to make an inconspicuous sign of the cross.

"Come over closer; put your arms around her," Sister Lucinie suggested.

Madame Vedrine did not stir. All she could see was that horrible open mouth.

"Don't be afraid."

Sister Pélagie thought that she herself would never have dared penetrate like that, deep into another's soul, as Sister Lucinie was doing, and she also thought that her companion's clear voice, never lowered or never raised to an unduly high pitch, was perfectly in keeping with the sad atmosphere of the room.

Madame Vedrine and she were whispering, but Sister Lucinie, who spoke as always in her natural voice, brought the terrified young woman over to touch the wrinkled forehead, made her implant a last kiss on the dead woman's face without showing any sign of revolt. It was Sister Lucinie who received the doctor and the priest, she, too, who made the mistress of the house stop to think, to make a note of addresses, to check names in the telephone book. And simultaneously she helped Sister Pélagie prepare the room for the last vigil. Then she telephoned the family, following the list made by the lady of the house, succeeded in getting in touch with Madame Vedrine's husband who had gone off with his relatives to town in the early morning, notified the other children of the dead woman, put out the holy water and the candles, placed Sister Pélagie and Madame Vedrine in two armchairs on either side of the bed, and served strong coffee to them. And when everything was done, she set off to town to hire some servants and knew exactly where to find them. Finally, when the first relatives arrived about six o'clock, she gave Sister Pélagie a sign that it was time to leave. Sister Pélagie admired her efficiency. Everything was in order.

Only one question remained unanswered in her mind. What did Sister Lucinie think of the unknown officer who had opened the door for her? But she had to live with her curiosity. Sister Lucinie never once referred to him.

Chapter IX

EACH NUN had brought a chair into the little courtyard which was so narrow and deep as to give the impression of being at the bottom of a well. No breath of air reached them, but there was no breeze on the terrace either, and the heat of the Sunday evening still lingered, along with the afterglow of the sunset, the stars sparkling overhead, and the blaring music of distant revelers. The nuns fanned themselves with pieces of cardboard, silent, waiting for a witticism from Sister Anne of the Cross or a laugh from Sister Perpétue.

"At this very moment," said Sister Jeanne, "they are arriving at the motherhouse."

"Yes, already I can hear the doorbell ring and hear old Sister Françoise: 'My dear Sister Dominique, my dear

Sister St. Jean.' She is turning from one to the other, throwing her arms around them and embracing them."

Sister Perpétue burst out laughing. "Poor Sister Françoise," she said with a comic inflection of her voice.

The scene awoke memories for each. They nostalgically recalled life in the motherhouse, but Sister Anne of the Cross, now acting Superior, did not allow their thoughts to dwell for long on the Mother General and the building they loved.

"Tomorrow," she said, "is washday. Sister Lucinie and Sister Pélagie will help the laundress to rinse and stretch the clothes. Sister Jeanne and Sister Perpétue will begin to spring-clean the house. No one has to go out, so we shall use the opportunity to shine up everything."

"And Sister Anne of the Cross will take charge of the kitchen and bake us a big cake, because all this work is going to make us very hungry by noon." Sister Perpétue did a perfect imitation of the old nun's voice, and the latter entered into the spirit of the joke.

"Sister Anne of the Cross will limit herself to boiling some vegetables that will offer no temptation to gluttony to the little ones entrusted to her care," she said.

"Sister Perpétue passes the store daily without buying candies. It is only proper to give some respite to a hungry soul, famished and hardened by trial."

The new voice was that of the chaplain. All the nuns laughed.

"Is that so?" Sister Jeanne asked. "What's so tough about such a trivial temptation?"

"Oh," Sister Perpétue answered in her most normal voice, "I'm not that sure that I wouldn't yield to it on certain days if I only had a franc. But the price of the candies reinforces the great strength of my conscience."

They felt like girls on vacation, free from Sister Dominique's strict supervision and Sister St. Jean's biting criticisms. They had dreaded falling under her thumb during the Mother Superior's absence, though none of them had ever said so openly.

This fear grew less after the old nun had been isolated but had not fully disappeared until it was announced that she was leaving with Sister Dominique for France. Sister Perpétue had expressed the universal satisfaction when she said to Sister Anne of the Cross the evening they left: "Sister, you have no idea how happy you are going to make us."

Sister Perpétue never hesitated to speak her mind. Her deep-seated simplicity and certainty of getting to heaven let her enjoy with a peaceful conscience pleasures the others denied themselves. She also had once experienced an extreme case of scruples, but this daughter of the Mediterranean among people from regions farther north accepted life more fatalistically than they did and yet managed to maintain her standing among them. The others loved her for her generosity, her easy manner, her gaiety, and a kind of immunity which her character ensured her and which more than once in thorny situations made it easy for her to win victories over the Mother Superior for the benefit of all. She often eased the conscience of the others by a straightforward expression of her satisfaction or admission of her weariness or annoyance, where the others felt obliged to hide their feelings. As a result, each of them got a clearer idea of her own strength and lost the feeling of being alone when she committed a fault or made a special effort, a sense of isolation that more than anything else undermined the desire for perfection shared by the four young women.

Sister Lucinie, in particular, loved Sister Perpétue's easy gaiety, but she felt herself unable to open up in the same way to every comer. For a whole month now she had felt a pang of discomfort every time she recalled the confidences she had given Sister Anne of the Cross, and this evening in particular her weakness made her feel miserable. These admissions had nevertheless helped her to recover an equilibrium and a certainty regarding her faith, but she felt she should have been able to reach these goals by herself. The anxiety she had then experienced now seemed to her to have lacked all adequate foundation, and she reproached herself as being guilty on two counts, for having made the confession and for having lacked the ability to think more clearly.

In addition, the admission of her doubts had brought a punishment. God had withdrawn from her. From that time she felt both freed and alone, remote from any superhuman destiny and again one of the anonymous crowd. "Sister Anne of the Cross psychoanalyzed me without knowing it," she thought as she fanned herself. But she was deceiving herself. Freed from this too heavy future, she now knew that there was no question of a nervous condition and that God really had descended on her, and remorse at having of her own will repelled Him overwhelmed her. She carried this regret with her everywhere. At times it diminished so as to be scarcely perceptible, but it never died out. This evening, when she had carried in her chair after the other nuns, when going with them to the chapel, she still experienced it, without feeling a grievance against Him. While she said her prayers, God appeared to be very far away and enveloped in a mist. It seemed to her that He was about to abandon her for good, and her weakness in the presence of the divine call made her feel infinitely ashamed.

"My God," she groaned.

Her voice re-echoed in the chapel, so heavy with sorrow in the midst of the general sense of well-being that it interrupted the prayers. The nuns turned to look at her and saw only the long, medieval sleeves of her habit hiding her face. At a sign from Sister Anne of the Cross, the recitation resumed, and when at nine o'clock they rose to go to their cells, a similar sign instructed them to leave Sister Lucinie in the warm solitude of the chapel. She was unaware either of her lamentation and resulting interruption of the prayers or of the departure of her companions.

"My God, come back to me," she prayed.

She could not survive any longer with the aid of prayers or of rules or of unburdening her problems in friendly ears. The only thing that remained was her desire to welcome God again, no matter what might be the unforeseeable obligations created by His presence, and she formulated this appeal hour after hour with complete abandon.

"My God, come back to me, even if I have to die."

She trembled with terror at the words she had pronounced, and still she repeated them, the resistance of

76

the flesh growing so violent that she dug her nails into the palms of her hands. The convulsive movement of her hands made her open her eyes, and the light combined with the physical pain to bring her back to an awareness of where she was. She blessed herself quickly and went upstairs. The clock on the landing told her it was five minutes to two. More silently and slowly than the night she closed her cell door behind her. Slipping her hand between the wardrobe and the wall, she produced a thick black moleskin wallet. She hid it here as a precaution, knowing that from time to time her cell was examined by uninvited visitors: Sister St. Jean certainly, Sister Dominique undoubtedly, and perhaps Sister Pélagie and Sister Anne of the Cross. It was against their network of curiosity or supervision that she erected this barrier.

She was not afraid of being punished, but she wrote there the poems she wanted to keep secret because they contained the reflection of all her emotions. No doubt they expressed her feelings imperfectly, perhaps even awkwardly, and often their serious flaws veiled her real attitude. For this reason among others she didn't want anyone to see them. She sat at the table, surprised by a great sob that overwhelmed her, and thought about the confessor at the motherhouse while she got out her pen. Having read some verses written by one of the novices, he first praised them for the ideas they expressed, then added: "The thought alone is not enough. Poetry requires an absolute perfection of form. It is better to express ourselves badly in prose than almost correctly in verse. It is close to sinful to write a bad poem."

Sister Lucinie nevertheless, in the secrecy of her cell, did sometimes write one when the need to do so became too strong.

> My heart is like a desert lake
> Of poisoned water.
> Nothing brightens the bleakness of its shore,
> Nor the anguish of its falls.
>
> Alone it flows downward to the port
> Of foreseen sin, stumbling about
> In uncertainty of effort.

The words scrawled on the page no longer said anything or conveyed any message. They could not free her. As a rule, when she composed a poem, a tremendous joy welled up in her, and if subsequently she always reread her poems with a sense of disappointment and discontent, the moment of creation raised her above her normal daily experience. Tonight there was no such result. She sat at her table, unable to find a way to improve the second verse and even lacking the desire to correct the rest. She regarded this as a spontaneous expression, subconscious rather than forced, and she looked for something in it to give her a better insight into her unknown self. She did not know how to meditate on herself or on God as she did on a material object or situation. She could not ally logic and abstraction, being satisfied with what she felt in this field. She made no effort to explain or understand. Even in her ordinary life, she felt more at home with intuition than with reflection, and it was precisely this ability to find the right answer intuitively that made her intellectually lazy, because it took care of her ordinary needs. She did not try to plumb her own depths or to learn the secrets of the unknown, even though she felt the urge.

"God does not appear in a particular shape," she usually told herself as an excuse. "He lets us imply His existence. If I affirm it, does this give me the right to look for Him? I don't dare penetrate the privacy of another, nor do I like my own intruded upon. Friendship should not commit any indiscretion if it wants to avoid becoming boring and disagreeable. What is the good of a need to know that reflects neither affection nor a solid faith?"

On this occasion she deliberately substituted the term "affection," for she had begun to doubt her love. All the happy flights of the past had persuaded her of the existence of a sentiment that supported a thousand small joyful sacrifices. She had built herself on this love. Every submission of her instincts was directed to God, every surrender of her self-willed and hasty temperament, every renunciation was based on this mutual love. But once the struggle was ended and habit had developed such an intensity that self-control no longer required effort, there was little occasion for frequent appeals to the divine help or outbursts of radiant thanks. Besides, Sister Lucinie believed that apart from any question of salvation, social life demanded the same self-denial and discipline in order to attain perfection, so that the idea of human obligation had replaced that of the supernatural. This new point of reference toned down still further the manifestations not of her affection but of her gratitude, and since she no longer acted for God but was rather content with words to establish and prove her love for

Him, she began to doubt the reality of a tenderness unsupported by any tangible proof.

She continued, nevertheless, to reflect as the night wore on, perhaps for the first time since she had come to the convent. I have relied too much on my feelings, she thought, using them to the limit. Now I must search again for God through my intelligence, if He will let me.

The clock outside struck three, and Sister Lucinie counted the strokes mechanically. They reverberated for some minutes in her head before she realized their meaning. The silence had become absolute, the distant music of the revelers having stopped without her realizing it. The entire town was asleep, yet Sister Lucinie did not feel the need for rest. She decided that Sister Anne's earlier decision to leave her behind in the chapel constituted a tacit authority to disobey the rule on sleep. Though the window was open on the terrace and the light was on, not a single mosquito buzzed around the electric bulb. She alone was awake. She . . .

She held her breath, suddenly attentive. Slowly the presence manifested itself. It suggested a weight on her shoulders, a call from behind like that of somebody staring intently. Sister Lucinie started to rise, then stopped with her fingers pressed against the edge of the table and her head half-turned on her shoulder. The atmosphere became dense as great waves swept down from the invisible. Each new current added to the weight pressing on the nun's body. A river of lead rolled down her damp temples over her shoulders, crushed by the load and her aching arms.

God was no longer behind but around her. She felt

Him everywhere, crowding in on her, pressing her against the walls, concentrating His very Self in a dominating and uncomprehended thought.

A pause in this development left the crushing mass weighing on her for an incalculable time. By a super-human effort, Sister Lucinie held out, unable and afraid to stir. A finger rested on her heart with a light disturbing touch.

"No," she breathed, "no, no, no."

For a second the finger stayed, then the tension less-ened. Slowly, in equally powerful waves, the presence withdrew, freed the air of the cell, and disappeared.

The tide had ceased to flow, and the fresh pungent fragrance of the trees was wafted in through the narrow window. Sister Lucinie leaned against the back of her chair and her hands fell wearily into her lap.

"That was too much for me, Lord," she murmured.

Chapter X

THEY CARRIED a heavy wicker basket, like a baby's crib, full of damp sheets. They had to pass through Sister Lucinie's room to reach the terrace, and they left the door open to hear Sister Perpétue singing.

They kept time to the song as they snapped the sheets with cracking noises to stretch them for hanging on the clothesline. The wind complicated the work. As they attached a sheet with clothes pins, it half blew away and fell back with a sharp noise, covering them in a cool mist that formed blue circles on their linen guimpes. Sister Pélagie laughed under the shower, letting go her hold on the sheets that Sister Lucinie held in a firm grip.

The morning's joy raised Sister Pélagie's spirits. She

wanted to sing a waltz tune to which she had danced long ago, and which, for no apparent reason, had kept ringing in her head ever since she got up. The day had a carnival air, even if she was not sure whether to attribute it to this dance tune that brought back for her the fragrance of the meadows, or to the sunlight that suggested the frothy gaiety of a country festival.

Everything lost its customary outlines, her thoughts flying away of their own accord into the clouds, dancing like butterflies in the sunlight, and peeping daringly down forbidden paths. She did not think of sin, nor did she think of God. Nothing remained but the freshness of damp fabrics, their sweeping white flights on the breeze, their noisy returns, the happy voice of Sister Perpétue and this invisible romance that sang within her heart. Today Sister Pélagie and her double had disappeared. Their place was taken by a stroll in the clouds, a desire to be free and even to revolt, not indeed against the rule but in such a way as to astonish Sister Anne of the Cross, to make Sister Perpétue laugh, to upset Sister Jeanne, or to provoke Sister Lucinie.

"Sister Lucinie," she asked, "were you ever in love?"

The words spurted so quickly from her mouth as to astonish her, and she felt a sudden sense of shame. She was afraid to look at the active figure in front of her squeezing once again the corners of the hems in which little pockets of water had accumulated. Sister Lucinie took no offense. The question seemed natural to her, and Sister Pélagie breathed more freely on hearing her calm answer.

"No, I have never loved any man except my father and my brothers, and the general love we have for everyone.

Apart from that, I truly believe I know nothing of what you mean by love."

Sister Pélagie followed with her eyes the careful movements of her companion. Her hands were unlike those of any of the others. Those of all seven nuns were pale, and except for Sister St. Jean and Sister Dominique, quite long-fingered, but none of them had fingers so strikingly tapered, with such a winged precision and speed in work. This quickness of movement did not make them less spiritual, rather they seemed animated by a soul of their own. It did, however, detract from their mysticism. Hands so slender and white should remain absolutely immobile, like those of a priest in an attitude of prayer. Action did not indeed demean them, although the previous life of Sister Lucinie had not prepared them for work, so that it might have seemed natural to find some awkwardness in them. But these familiar movements and this humble work so diligently performed seemed to lower them to a very average religious and intellectual level, out of keeping with their appearance.

It seemed to Sister Pélagie that this revealed a certain spiritual poverty. The word poverty did not quite express what she had in mind. She did not think that Sister Lucinie was capable of doing anything improper or mean. But she thought that the veil of silence that had covered this nun for several months was a little absurd and fitted badly with the skill she displayed in manual tasks. Her refusal to express what she was thinking should normally lead to reflection and concentration. Constant manual work, however, did not favor meditation, or at least so Sister Pélagie thought, for her own dreams weak-

84

ened her ability to work, while, on the other hand, when she became immersed in work, she could not think of anything except what she was doing. Of course, certain habitual motions, which had become reflex, sometimes permitted her thoughts to wander on another level, but Sister Pélagie seldom reached that state. Her existence was divided between the dream, which represented for her the only form of meditation, and manual work. Others, she thought, should experience the same sort of incompatibility.

She always judged others by comparison with herself, and if she did not consciously regard herself as superior to those around her, she considered a thing to be good to the extent to which it fitted her own attitudes. In these terms, Sister Lucinie's silence offended her sociability. She could understand it as an element in a static life devoted entirely to prayer, for while she herself had abandoned this type of religious life in favor of a purely imaginary existence, she still believed that contemplation was the road to sanctity. Since her companion's silence was not complemented by the other elements she believed she had a logical right to demand, Sister Pélagie judged this voluntary restraint as humiliating to the rest of the community. Undoubtedly, Sister St. Jean's insinuations played a part in these conclusions, but they did no more than confirm the sense of annoyance Sister Pélagie felt in Sister Lucinie's company. The trend of her evolution suggested a desire for self-improvement and an effort to acquire sanctity. Each of the nuns interpreted Sister Lucinie's purpose differently, according to her personality. Only the incorrigibly good-humored Sister Perpétue regarded it with indifference. Sister St. Jean had criticized it openly. Sister Jeanne admitted that it made her uneasy.

"I cannot pass near her without feeling afraid," the latter had said as she went to get the milk. "Haven't you noticed? She anticipates your words and often answers a question before you have formulated it."

Sister Pélagie was not afraid of Sister Lucinie. Rather, she experienced annoyance, a confused feeling in which envy was mixed with shame, for not following the same difficult path. This shame expressed itself in a deep-seated desire to see her companions stagnate at the same level as herself. Everything that outstripped Sister Pélagie spiritually offended her.

This morning, in the bright sunlight, she bore her companion a grudge for not having been annoyed by her question. Such imperturbability filled her with a deep contempt for Sister Jeanne's views no less than for Sister Lucinie's temperament.

"Love," said Sister Pélagie aloud, "allows you no calm. You admire, you want to be the first, you hope to receive all the joys and some of the sorrows, you wish to sacrifice yourself, you go to the point of giving the most lavish gifts, but on condition that your conduct is known, for behind the one you love you always find self-love. You want to get back everything you give and even more, because you are sure, when one of your thoughts wanders toward something else, that it betrays nothing; while you do not experience a like certainty as regards your lover, and you insist on him giving his entire self."

"In all of this," Sister Lucinie asked, "what place do you keep for those around you?"

86

"A very small corner. The well-hidden service stairway of a fine mansion. The two who are in love remain alone at the center of the universe, and the others allow them to go on living."

Sister Lucinie took the basket and went back down into the courtyard. It was a very tiny area with a concrete floor, crowded with potted flowers and the big basins in which the laundress steeped and scrubbed the wash. A depressing damp odor clung to it, and this atmosphere was reflected on the faces of the two women while they wrung the towels dry and piled them in the basket.

Sister Lucinie was unable to speak her mind more fully to this near stranger, but she turned over silently her definition of love, comparing it with what she herself experienced, and she seemed to be penetrating into a desert because what she discovered in herself lacked pith, enthusiasm, and any quality of explosiveness. Sister Pélagie's deep and sibilant voice continued to ring in her ears: "The service stairway of a fine mansion." She had taken this stairway and enlarged it into a stairway of honor, a royal road used by all those whom it was her duty to serve, and her concern was concentrated principally on them and not on the loved one hidden in the depths of the palace. She had learned to suppress her feeling of nausea when cleaning up filth, to prepare the meals in joy, to leave her prayers with a smile to bring pleasure to others. And not only had she not been able to reach her loved one, but He scorned her when she asked too insistently.

She was not envious of Sister Pélagie, rather she forgot her and thought only of her words. Already these words had taken on the universality and impersonality of old texts read and reread without reference to the author. She was reflecting on an experience quite different from her own, and she went back mentally into the past to try to find out if she, at the moment she had entered the convent or at some other time, had known this dedicated self-centeredness. But no matter where she looked, she always found in herself the same tranquillity of mood that she experienced at this very moment. The main thing had been to serve others, following her natural bent, not merely a sense of goodness but a belief in an obligation toward misfortune and toward the world. She had not developed a formal theory about this, still less had she deduced it from a principle. All she did was to pay the debt of happiness. And now, she thought, all this calm seemed insipid when compared with what Sister Pélagie had to say.

"And so," Sister Pélagie repeated in a low voice when they found themselves back again and alone on the sunlit terrace, "you have never loved anyone?"

"No. Not in the way you described, and not any man. I have a feeling that I only half love. I know nothing of those great emotional flights you mentioned. I knew, you understand, that Sister Dominique's presence gave me pleasure. I felt well when I was near her, but I was not conscious of my affection until the day she was leaving, when her departure grieved me."

"Yes," commented Sister Pélagie with disdain, "your heart beats slow and your soul is asleep."

She had stopped working to lean casually on the low brick wall that separated the terrace from the neighboring houses. She studied with curiosity Sister Lucinie's face as it appeared and disappeared rapidly in time with her work. Although she was approaching thirty and was wrapped in a habit that was too big for her and a huge blue apron, her body had flexibility and an enviable elegance. Sister Pélagie told herself that a vigorous man could rouse this tall girl slumbering in her chastity and in her pastel emotions.

"No doubt about it," she murmured to herself, "the heat is getting me down."

She registered the thought with amusement, and a wave of pugnaciousness took hold of her. She wanted to stir Sister Lucinie's anger and indignation, to provoke a quarrel as a way to wound her companion and gain a victory over her. Nevertheless, this impulse remained hidden. She lacked courage to bring it straight out. She feared Sister Anne of the Cross, who watched over them from her place in the kitchen. Everyone was aware of the strength of the acting Superior and the extreme severity hidden under her normal good humor. Sister Dominique had shown the strength of her intervention when Sister St. Jean was isolated, and one thing that Sister Pélagie most definitely did not want was to be sent to the motherhouse. She knew today that she was going to leave the convent, but she would do so of her own accord and in her own time. She was determined to avoid a scolding and punishment.

Sister Lucinie continued to spread the clothes on the line, turning over in her mind her companion's last remark. The intention to wound escaped her. What she saw was a diagnosis of a situation, and she could not deny its accuracy, all the more because it expressed what she had felt for a long time. The calm atmosphere of the convent, by letting her live exactly the kind of life she loved, had wrapped her not indeed in a routine existence, for she had learned how to absorb the latest and most modern medical techniques, to adapt herself to the wishes of the different doctors in the town, to improvise by herself when an urgent need arose, and often to take the place of the physician when the poverty of the sick people prevented them from calling him, but in a machine-like procedure in which the correct reaction occurred almost unconsciously. At the beginning, during her apprenticeship, she had reflected on her life, but now she lived it too perfectly. It had ceased to involve effort.

The unaccustomed silence of Sister Pélagie and the empty basket brought her back from her thoughts. She looked with concern at the young woman who was sitting down swinging her legs, and suddenly realized that she was no longer helping in the work.

"Are you tired, Sister Pélagie?"

Sister Pélagie studied with some malice the sad eyes fixed on her.

"It's nothing. I simply find myself in a state that favors the commission of sin, and I take advantage of your untiring activity to enjoy my idleness."

Sister Lucinie smiled.

"A rose-colored temptation?" she asked.

"No," Sister Pélagie giggled, "rather a red temptation smelling of sulphur."

Her eyelids did not flicker as she returned Sister Lucinie's questioning look. There was no opportunity for further words between them, for they had begun to go back down for another basket of linen. Sister Pélagie again experienced doubt as to the wisdom of expressing her nervous condition, but Sister Lucinie was already alerted by the tone of voice and tried to grasp the danger revealed by her words. As a general rule, she was quick to recognize a bad mood in any of the nuns and the underlying cause of their melancholy. Today, she had been slower to see Sister Pélagie's anger, because her excessive introspection had dulled the extraordinary receptive instrument that was her body.

Should she sacrifice herself for the other, she reflected, and once more interrupt the inner search that every slight incident forced her to suspend? For a moment she regretted her choice, thinking that a contemplative order would have been better for her spiritual life. This was the only debate between her conscience, entreating more time for recollection, and her desire to help Sister Pélagie. The sure intuition that normally guided her did not come to her aid right away, but her annoyance remained hidden under a blank exterior. She merely experienced a sense of discomfort without knowing the exact cause, while the two of them filled the basket. Then they were back again on the rose-colored terrace. Now Sister Pélagie was spreading the linen, seeking in vain for some way to resume the conversation.

Everything suddenly seemed empty and dangerous to her. She was risking her entire salvation, day after day, because of mental sloth. She was plunging herself into her romantic dreams as into a soothing bath, and this was now reacting like a drug. She felt herself poisoned by the unreal love that fermented in her mind and in her body. Though she loved no actual person, her flesh vibrated in secret under the stress of the hot desert wind. She got up in the morning with a never-satisfied sense of anticipation, entertained yet deceived by the over-dainty images of her dreams. Today the shell was cracking, and she was fully aware that the crisis had been induced by what she had witnessed the previous afternoon.

"Sister Lucinie," she asked, "do you know the officer who opened Madame Vedrine's door?"

Sister Lucinie also had been waiting for the conversation to be resumed. She had been thinking of the long spell of work they had endured all through the winter and spring and on into the summer which was already half over, and of the isolation of the little community far from any strong spiritual aid, balancing these elements against the amorous passion that Sister Pélagie had confessed. She felt that her companion's discouragement paralleled her own fears and hesitations, and that because she lacked hope or support she was letting herself slide down the slope of bewilderment. Sin was hypnotizing her. Sister Lucinie had not dared speak, unsure of her own presentments, and waiting for her companion to make the next move.

"He is young Madame Vedrine's lover," Sister Pélagie continued. "I saw them day before yesterday in a situation that left no doubt, when I was searching the house for someone to help me after the grandmother died."

If Sister St. Jean, Sister Jeanne, or even Sister Anne of the Cross had been the one to whom this remark was confided, the conversation would have degenerated into a light gossip that would have calmed and satisfied Sister Pélagie's emotional commitment. But Sister Lucinie saw everything from a distinct viewpoint. She wore out her listeners by comments that turned the conversaion from its normal direction.

"You must have been very, very upset," she said.

"I took an instant dislike to them," Sister Pélagie admitted. "And then the obvious fear expressed in her voice, her way of adjusting her dressing gown, which made her seem so childish, her languor . . . I assure you, I forgave her right away and I understood, for God alone knows what I myself would have done in her place. Do I shock you?"

"A little. It seems to me I could never have reacted like that."

Sister Pélagie laughed softly. "But I am a woman, Sister Lucinie. You are just a beautiful mechanical doll. We were both reaching the same conclusion on that score just now. Don't look at me like that. The most surprising thing in that day's experience is not this first episode itself, still less my reflections on it, but the contrast between that moment and the one when Madame Vedrine reappeared in the death room. Do you recall her absolutely correct behavior? A dark dress, absence of make-up, black stockings. She respected, probably not the dead woman, but death itself."

"She respected God," Sister Lucinie interrupted gently.

"God? Possibly," Sister Pélagie agreed after a moment's hesitation. "To be exact, one fears and respects death because God appears in its shadows. But now my surprise increases. I want to stress these differences of attitudes, on the one side sin and on the other the most complete respect, extending even to matters of etiquette. Moreover, she gave the impression of sincerity. Do you think that the one element can compensate for the other?"

Instead of answering her question, Sister Lucinie asked a totally different one.

"Who is the man you are in love with?"

Sister Pélagie was flabbergasted.

"Who? I?" She wiped her damp forehead mechanically with the wet towel she held in her hand. "I'm not talking about myself."

"But you are," Sister Lucinie insisted. "By pure chance you blab out these secrets to me, because Sister Anne of the Cross chose me to help you in this work. Perhaps you would have preferred another of the sisters, but unfortunately I am the one. You talk to me in this way because you count on my discretion and you look for help against yourself. How can I help you if you insist on hiding half the truth? You tell me the story because it parallels your own situation. You'd prefer a diagnosis in the third person. But don't you think it would be better to come right out in the open?"

"I assure you I don't love any man. I don't know any well enough for that. I dream, I tell myself stories, I play a little game." Sister Pélagie blushed, not because of the admission of lack of control over her senses, but because such fictions seemed very childish for her age. "I love nobody in the true sense of the word."

"Nevertheless, you do believe in God?"

They were now gathering the heavy calico bedspreads, which had become stiff through drying out too quickly, and folding them. The task joined their hands, separated them, and brought them close again in turn, and they conducted the conversation through the waving white barrier. They knew they were alone. Sister Perpétue's song was fading in the distance, and Sister Anne of the Cross was banging pots around in the kitchen.

"Yes, I do believe in Him," Sister Pélagie declared quite definitely. "I believe in Him desperately, but I do not love Him. I don't mean to say that I detest Him, but I can't find any lovable aspect. What element can I isolate in Him without immediately bringing to light that ungraspable infinity that nobody can comprehend? And if I do succeed in isolating one element, if, for example, I choose Jesus, Jesus does not answer. And as I told you, love exists for me only if I receive it in return."

"Didn't it ever occur to you that your weakness might be the cause of God's silence rather than the result?"

Sister Pélagie shook her head in denial. She finally felt a need to concentrate and tell the truth. Her animosity decreased. Sister Lucinie's voice and presence had served as an unexpected reminder of the peace of the mother-house. The young woman revived the helpful and mystical atmosphere of the old convent. Her presence, which a moment before had been irritating, now served to calm Sister Pélagie, who found herself drawn by this subtle power.

"My neglect does not cause God's indifference. He never took any notice of me, even in the novitiate, when His presence in the chapel stirred me very deeply. At that time I was aware of Him. My faith revealed Him at every turn. Now, so far away, I sink ever deeper into my own loneliness and weakness, into my poor excuses. I still believe in Him. While I talk to you, He becomes real as He did before. The only difference is that I have told myself a thousand times that my conduct cannot disturb His order. Day by day I have cut down on my prayers and expressions of love hoping to resume all of them later on. Nevertheless, all these lapses have not separated me completely from Him. I believe without hoping. I know that I am straying to the outside border of His kingdom. I have never used my strength, and to-day this strength seems to me sterile. I believe I shall never reform."

"What you are looking for primarily is something to force you to act," Sister Lucinie said. "You know that God demands everything of you and that you should not wait for an express message, a communication spelled out in our terms. He can bring us peace, but He will not speak to you as I am speaking, except as a special grace. God once became man, like us, but He has returned to His own stature and is now for us only the unknown. We know nothing about Him in spite of the progress of science which can make judgments or express opinions only about a few elements, in spite of the visions of a few privileged souls, in spite of the sacred scripture.

"The fact that St. Teresa or St. John of the Cross could communicate nothing to us about God does not mean that He is obscure. It simply means that in their ecstasy they experienced only a particularly vivid joy and not knowledge, or that such knowledge as they obtained was so removed from our human experience that no word from our speech could translate it. Nevertheless, we must not describe it as obscure. Let us rather recognize that our senses are too imperfect to see the light. Let us resign ourselves to live on His circumference and love Him as He wishes. God, even if unknown, remains God."

"I know that God exists," Sister Pélagie protested, "but I have become enmeshed through my own choice and I lack the will to free myself."

"Then why do you ask my help?"

"Because I know that I am doing wrong. The last vestiges of my good will serve to warn me that I am sliding down the slope. I expect nothing of myself and everything of others, in a detached way. I have grown indifferent."

"That's not true," Sister Lucinie replied with feeling. "Nothing leaves you indifferent, and this silence that you affect is false. God holds you through your remorse. You shelter Him just as you shelter Satan."

She had gripped her companion's wrists as she spoke, and those long fingers which a moment ago had seemed to Sister Pélagie unsuited for any physical exertion now held her as in a vise.

"God made you a woman, doubly pure in your body and in your education, and He guaranteed you freedom from defilement by your religious habit. And through laziness you are leaving Him. You say that He does not speak to you, but read the gospel again and there you will find all that it is possible for man to understand about God, for if we do not know what He is, at least we know how to act so that we can raise ourselves toward Him."

Suddenly Sister Lucinie changed her tone, and released her grip with a little gesture of displeasure. "Stop," she said. "You are hurting me."

Amazed, Sister Pélagie massaged her right wrist on which could be seen the white marks of Sister Lucinie's fingers.

"But it was you had a hold of me," she said with tears in her eyes. She rubbed her arm, her gaze still fixed on her companion. It seemed to her that the expression on that face would never change, that she could not continue to bear the sight of those trembling lips. Although she believed that she herself was a vile creature, she had not imagined that she could possibly provoke such a reaction in another.

"Sister!" she begged.

Earlier that morning she had wanted to arouse her companion's anger and make her feel this scorn, when the sheets had been flapping in the wind like flags and spreading noisily around them a fresh drizzle like a champagne mist, when the foolish intoxication of her heart reflected the gaiety of her surroundings. But the scorn itself had blotted out her joy.

For the second time in a few days Sister Pélagie noticed a kind of change in Sister Lucinie's appearance. It resulted neither from her bearing nor her words. The burning and disturbing face of the silent nun was not what called attention, but rather the transparency of her skin and the luminosity of her eyes.

"Sister," Sister Pélagie begged once more.

"Please forgive me," Sister Lucinie said in a low tone. "I have been blaming you and I am no better than you." She laid a light and loving hand on her companion's shoulder. "God is there, I can assure you that He is coming, but He calls on us to live always beyond our own strength. He sets for us a degree of perfection that must always be surpassed, must each day be higher than the day before. He demands of us a difficult life, and we are all alike in our fear of exceeding our capabilities, because we despair of loving Him — for we do love Him, and I can assure you that He exists."

Sister Lucinie was talking to Sister Pélagie, but she was persuading herself. Her arguments came from a source other than her soul. She pronounced the words which she would have liked to have heard from Sister

98

Anne of the Cross. She reached the very conclusion that she herself had rejected the previous evening in God's presence, and yet she did not have the courage to submit herself to it.

"It is so good to be alive," she moaned wordlessly in a mental prayer. "I fear death so dreadfully. Why do I love this body to which I give no attention? Why do I feel sorry for this heart that serves me without my being aware of it, for this blood and these muscles and all the things that surround me? Why should I attach myself to them with such fear and so possessively, since I enjoy them only in the very moment in which I fear to lose them? Why, Lord, should I run away from you when in fact my desire is to lose myself in your infinity?"

Sister Pélagie withdrew a step from her companion and awoke her from her reverie.

"Sister," she said, "I have felt your peace pass into me. I believe in God and through you I shall return to Him. Let me lean a little longer on your strength."

"It is not my strength or my peace," Sister Lucinie protested, "but God's peace and God's strength. Only He can communicate Himself to you. I am merely an instrument."

They carried the loaded basket down into the small room and spread the linen on the table.

"He possesses me," Sister Lucinie repeated to herself in terror. "I am helpless against Him. Even though I refuse Him, I cannot repulse Him. The others are aware of it even when I am not."

Chapter XI

MOTHER ST. AUGUSTINE, who had charge of the parish school, did not maintain regular contact with the community of the nursing sisters. In the town she enjoyed the reputation of possessing great authority over souls and of being able to persuade young girls quickly to choose the religious life. On two separate occasions she had succeeded in switching girls who had decided to enter the nursing sisters to her own order, and she assumed that Sister Dominique was not likely to pardon such actions very easily.

As a matter of fact, the old sister had never learned about it, but Mother St. Augustine preferred to enjoy her triumph at a distance from her victim. Once Sister Dominique had left she thought that it was proper to go in person and survey the scene. She wanted to profit from this absence to lead the five women who had been left behind toward a higher spiritual life. In her opinion the chaplain's intelligence was limited, his sermons were infantile, and his zeal lacked drive.

And so one afternoon in August she found herself seated in the little reception room on La Fontaine Street, surrounded by the five nuns, like a queen on her throne. This comparison sprang to her mind when she noticed the circle of five starched guimpes, their owners leaning forward in an attitude of respect not always evident in her own community. She wound up an indirect criticism of the chaplain and waited with some concern for audience reaction, but there was none. They listened politely, hands joined on their knees, pale faces slightly lowered like delicate flowers. She was struck by their frailty. One did not find such faces among her own daughters.

"It seems to me," she said in a voice that expressed a judgment, "that you subject yourselves to unduly severe fasts, incompatible with the active life you lead. And that is particularly true in your case, Sister Lucinie."

Sister Lucinie turned the question aside with a quiet gesture, but the others looked at each other with startled glances, rather like school children surprised by their teacher in an escapade.

"You must look after your health," Mother St. Augustine insisted. "The low esteem in which one should bear one's body must not make one forget that it is the Lord's work."

They listened to the deep voice, occasionally interrupted without warning by a shrill tone. The Reverend

101

Mother's thick tongue seemed to swallow entire syllables or weigh them down with guttural aspirations. She took pride in dragging out overlong sentences, scattering around her an unending flow of commonplace remarks that covered a series of unconnected subjects, passing from the question of food to the difficulties of maintaining supplies, from supplies to the communists, and so on. Sister Perpétue sat in open-mouthed amazement, missing completely the comic side of it.

"No," Sister Lucinie interrupted boldly, "it is not the communists who destroy Christianity. An institution collapses when it no longer fulfills a social need or when its members are rotten to the core. Thank God we have not reached that point, and we shall continue to live, because human nature needs a morality that thinks little of the stomach and of human logic, and it needs a religion that will raise its eyes above that level.

"If we go on thinking that the enemy is outside, we shall precipitate Christianity into a sewer in which it will smother. The evil is in those of us who accept watchwords extraordinarily similar to those given by the other side, who speak of nothing but war and censures and hatred. Where does one find the universal love of the Sermon on the Mount, the readiness to turn the other cheek, the love of martyrdom that inspired the early Christians, or the ascetic ideals of Elias? Where . . . "

"Sister Lucinie," said Sister Anne of the Cross, interrupting her, "you are straying."

The young nun stopped abruptly. She looked, in turn, with eyes aflame at the nun who had interrupted her and at Mother St. Augustine. A violent anger boiled up inside her against all these women installed in their religion as in a comfortable armchair, who thought they were fully protected from mortal sin through the sole fact of being baptized and having the faith. She was tempted to continue her diatribe, but a picture suddenly placed itself between her and her words. This was not the formless vision she had experienced about a week earlier, when she had felt an unbearable threat build itself up within her, but one of those sun-steeped gospel scenes that she used to bring into focus by dwelling on incidents in the life of Christ. Jesus appeared to her writing on the ground and saying: "Let him who is without sin cast the first stone . . . "

Only a few months earlier she had found her life as a nun in this peaceful white house an easy matter. And today, without being aware of the distance she had fallen, she was abandoning herself to one of the fits of anger of her earlier life, and to the desire to gain a victory over an adversary and wound her self-esteem.

"I'm sorry," she said in a low tone. "I was wrong."

"But not at all, my dear child," Mother St. Augustine assured her in her most wheedling tones, "you were absolutely right. Our principal enemies, for Christians like ourselves who are strong in the faith, are within us. But for the mass of those in doubt, who lack knowledge, the outside enemy, the one who forbids even the mention of God's name . . . "

The curious guttural rhythms of her voice grated on Sister Lucinie's nerves, but the Superior of the parish school had her at her mercy. Mother St. Augustine now felt the need to go over her entire argument from the beginning and to establish for her reverend audience the overwhelming correctness of her position. She also enjoyed curbing this untamed spirit before her. A college graduate indeed, she thought with bitter satisfaction, while she dragged out her speech, inflecting her sentences like a mission preacher in the pulpit.

Sister Lucinie sat in front of her, slightly bowed, apparently attentive, but gradually forcing herself to hear the words, stubbornly repeating her prayers to calm her annoyance and escape toward God. Then, without realizing it, she stopped praying in order to examine the fault she had committed.

"I am letting myself go because things are so easy," she thought. "I have reached a plateau above which I must rise. Since I find no hardship in keeping the rule, I should practice greater austerity and deny myself every pleasure in order to bring myself to endure the thought of death and destroy the violent need to live I now feel. I should meditate more, try to find out why God now terrifies me when previously He seemed to me the Master of all the world's sweetness. In death I can fear only two things, the suffering that precedes it and the unknown that follows it."

"Sister Lucinie, you live in another world."

The directress of the parish school was standing before her, her hand stretched out, her head slightly bowed, her eyes looking up like a goat about to attack.

Sister Lucinie realized that she had followed the others into the corridor and that she was so immersed in her thoughts as to have completely put Mother St. Augustine out of her head.

"I am sorry," she repeated. "It's so hot."

"I think you dream too much," the hostile voice said. "Those who like you are active in the world should not let themselves dream. I wonder just how far modern ideas have contaminated you, and you can be sure that I shall discuss the matter with your Superior General."

"I think," Sister Anne of the Cross interrupted, "that we are well able to keep an eye on her, and that you would overstep the bounds if you interfered. I am in charge of this house."

"Of course, of course, Sister, I have absolutely no intention of interfering. Nevertheless, I repeat, dreams are dangerous for a nun."

"She will write to her, I know she will write to her," Sister Perpétue cried in terror, the moment the door shut behind the visitor. "Sister Lucinie, what's going to happen to us?"

"Nothing whatsoever," Sister Anne of the Cross answered irritably. "Our Mother General will believe me rather than her."

"What difference does it make?" Sister Lucinie asked. "If she writes, it will affect only me, and if our Mother believes that I was wrong, it is better for me that she should know it."

"What a mischievous person," said Sister Jeanne.

Sister Lucinie noticed that they were all gathered around her in a state of loving concern, unable to help, but ready to sustain her with their love, ruled by a sense of community that commanded them to take her part against any outsider.

This was her family, the basis of her security. Nevertheless, she felt alone, for this flock of startled swallows could not defend her in her interior struggle. On the contrary, they increased it and caused her anguish without wishing to do so. Still, it was good to feel them around her, as it would be good at the moment of death to listen to their prayers and their helpless sorrow, for on that day also she would find them around her and still be alone in her passage across the one-way bridge. Neither their faith nor their big, fluttering cornettes could protect her then. One had to take that step for oneself, as well as bear the pain that preceded it, and she knew that she would bear it without any show of emotion, true to the code of her middle-class family in which evidences of fear and pain betrayed a lack of breeding and were consequently hidden under a veil of silence and apparent unconcern. And then she would face what followed. She was not really frightened very much about the judgment. She hoped to go directly to God without any punishment, though without having any clear idea of how this would be accomplished. Would she dissolve in God and lose her individuality? She believed in an obscure way that this moment would come quickly, and accordingly the only thing that remained, creating and supporting her fear of God which was stronger than her desire to experience ecstasy, was the animal terror of death. This she could hide but could not destroy, even if she submitted herself absolutely to God's will.

She was standing with her back to the white partition, surrounded by the nuns whose presence she had forgotten. The light penetrated the corridor from the courtyard through a window over the door covered by a green curtain, bathing them in soft and warm pastel shades. Sister Lucinie was conscious of a presence through a slight catch in the upper part of her chest, a sense of pressure. Then a gentle flowering like the bursting of a liquid bubble welled up within her. She felt the presence rest for a moment on her shoulders and her neck before disappearing.

The touch of Sister Anne of the Cross's rough hand brought her back to earth. "Daughter," the old nun was whispering, "daughter." Sister Perpétue brought a chair on which Sister Pélagie and Sister Jeanne helped her to seat herself.

Their affection did not destroy the memory of the other contact. She bent her neck to feel once more this weight, to get a taste of the joy that was near but that had not taken possession of her. This time, at least, in the speed of the sensation, her body had not revolted, but yet her submission had not been joyous.

The four nuns stood looking at her, compelled to silence by the brightness in the eyes and the joined hands. Nevertheless, Sister Perpétue was not able to hold her emotion.

"Sister Lucinie," she asked, "what's happening to you? I was sure that you were dying."

"I really don't know."

And that was true. The memory rapidly faded away. She was almost beginning to doubt that she had had this sudden and fleeting experience, and still the fear revived within her. She peered into the deepening gloom of the evening.

Chapter XII

SISTER LUCINIE studied Sister Perpétue sorrow-
fully. The tiny nun looked like a child as she exclaimed
over the pink radishes spread out and chopped into
pieces and the beets with their huge white stems and
luxuriant green leaves. As she surveyed them, she played
with a pat of fresh butter that she was about to drop
into a bowl of cold water. Her longing to take Sister
Lucinie's place showed itself principally in the way she
admired the vegetables, the sight of which brought to
life in her imagination the nearby countryside she was
never able to visit.

The five women were this evening assembled in the
kitchen, and Sister Lucinie knew that they were all keeping an eye on her, particularly Sister Anne of the Cross,

whom she had noticed looking very hard at her while giving an order the meaning of which she did not understand. Sister Perpétue's frail hands called for rest, but those of Sister Jeanne and Sister Pélagie were equally thin. They reminded Sister Lucinie of disembodied beings, floundering about in a semi-stupor, simultaneously requesting and refusing a task she could not abandon to them.

"I'm sorry, Sister Perpétue, I don't think I should let you take over for me," Sister Lucinie said.

"Of course not." The tiny nun smiled graciously. "I didn't mean to ask you. Forgive my exclamation."

Sister Lucinie did not notice the pleasure of the acting Superior. Sister Perpétue was the one the community tended to spoil, and her companion felt guilty at refusing her this pleasure, particularly as there seemed to be little reason for her attitude. She thought it hid some sort of selfishness, not knowing what future design excused her conduct. But absorbed in her many tasks, she could not reflect on the matter until time for prayer arrived.

The chapel represented a haven of safety, a chosen place where contacts with God adjusted themselves to her level. In this room, perfumed and adorned by the pious efforts of the women, replete with prayers and with memories of tears and of smiles, Sister Lucinie was able to reflect, to humble herself and love God, without fearing the silent, invisible, and undefined force whose infinity at times closed in on her without losing its extension, showing itself like a dense night, and leaving a memory of the impossible.

When face to face with this divine manifestation, the young woman lost control of herself under the weight of fear. Her reason disappeared to such an extent that she felt her body was waiting only for a struggle in which it would inevitably be overcome, but overcome through persuasion. In a knowledge consisting entirely of impressions, Sister Lucinie realized that she must accept, but still she resisted, and her refusal seemed to her as inexplicable as her perception. She attributed it to the fear of death, but since at that moment she no longer experienced this fear, she consequently forgot the quality of the related anguish. For God was able to control her own terror and communicate it to her as an experience unconnected with earthly life.

This vague foreknowledge of the divine essence seemed to Sister Lucinie like a sin of pride. She could not accept an interpretation that singled her out from all the others for a direct association with God. She found nothing in her past conduct to justify such a supernatural choice. What had she to offer other than this charity that carried her along with no more choice than that of a log tossed about in a swollen flood, than this love for others that flowed from her like a perfume from a flower, and these prayers that sang of an interior joy which came from God and returned to God? All of this scarcely called for action on her part, as though her body, her heart, and her hands served to hold prisoner the willing perfection of another soul, while her intelligence examined and questioned coldly, in search of certainty.

The duality of her formal education and of her religious training paralyzed her, demanding mathematical definitions of the lyric and loving outpouring of prayer. She was as suspicious of the kind of remorse that her psychology professor would have attributed to a glandular deficiency, as she was of the joy that was perhaps attributable to her excellent health. In consequence, she found no way to choose between the spiritual quality of her own experience and the materialism of a half-forgotten science.

Her understanding of God had developed from her early childhood, something that preceded conscious judgment, then was in turn accepted, denied, and reaffirmed by an act of the will overcoming the doubt of the mind. After an aggressive rejection between the ages of eighteen and nineteen, she had again experienced a desire for God, not by a call of the intelligence for a more certain justice or a protecting power, but by her faith in things unseen.

Rejecting logical skepticism that crushed life and destroyed all mystery, she turned in the direction of the unknown, yielding at first to the great temptation of surrealism, to the need to know and demonstrate its truth and originality, and to discover again above the level of the unconscious a destiny directed from without. But recognizing in herself as an outstanding characteristic this definite leaning toward purity, gentleness, and goodness, she had been sufficiently sincere to go to the extreme limit of liberty, not by rejecting all restraints in order to achieve total self-expression, but by accepting a rule of life common to many women where these attitudes might blossom anonymously.

As she saw it, there was little to distinguish her from her companions. Her work at least was only slightly better, her ability to pray but little more developed. She observed silence only a shade more than the rule obliged, and her self-mastery surpassed the common level by a scarcely perceptible fraction. At best, these virtues separated her only marginally from the group and were not such as to raise her above it. She knew neither the ingenuousness of Sister Perpétue, the evocative power and emotion of Sister Pélagie, nor the inexhaustible patience of Sister Jeanne.

A fear of sinning against humility threatened Sister Lucinie's sincerity, making her hesitate to accept the divine choice offered her, and even preventing her from following fully the ascetic line of conduct that shaped itself within her almost without intervention of her will. A line of conduct in which each prayer, each fast, and each work, pointing toward an unattainable perfection, called for further prayers, further fasts, and further works.

This lack of faith in herself recalled in a strange way the emotional uncertainties of her youth, but now God, the real presence of God, checked every refusal and made it impossible even to present the problem clearly. She wanted to know a divine essence that neither her own experience nor that of others made clear for her. The unknown became still further unknown when she asked herself this question — who am I to merit such a choice? It conjured up in her mind a rather absurd picture — that of a nun in a cornette, a stocking stretched on a darner in her left hand, a needle in the right, cutting with her teeth the thread wrapped around her fingers.

Just that, Sister Lucinie thought ironically as she looked at this caricature of herself, a working ant, an ant that stops before its hole, looks at an immense lake that fills the valley, and asks — what am I? Surprised that it has nothing else to do except to fill the granaries, it imagines a more spectacular function for itself if God remembers it. But it is only an ant, and I am only a woman. If God pauses in my presence, I should not seek in this a significance it does not possess, but merely bow myself before His will without attempting to discover some hidden logic.

Shaking her head, the young woman pushed aside the picture that kept returning to her mind, and found herself in the chapel where the light penetrated in undulating waves. A cool breeze blew through the open windows, making the candles flicker and caressing the bowed heads and drying the temples of the women deep in prayer. Sister Perpétue suddenly sighed, shaking off a load. Sister Lucinie recalled her words: "How wonderful to live in the country!"

Each morning for the past three days a light cart, perched high on its narrow wheels, had carried Sister Lucinie to a farmhouse just outside the town. The nun enjoyed the deep-toned richness of the earth, the high-pitched song of the cicadas, the warbling of the birds in the olive trees and the pines, and the monotonous clip-clop of the mare. She loved the brown path that snaked between the spreading vines, passing occasionally under a solitary tree, resin-perfumed and re-echoing the whispers of cooing doves, to reveal at length, at the top of a hill, the house with rose-colored roof and golden walls nestling in a fold of the ground like a jewel in the palm of a warm human hand.

She discovered the blue round-shouldered mountains of Algeria, the harsh plains where a few scattered pine trees broke the monotony of dark stubble or of vineyards with receding lines of vines, green against the red earth, from which rose bright, wavy layers of steaming air.

For three years she had lived in this country without knowing anything other than the soulless town with its narrow streets. The lonely, flamboyant, and hostile countryside lifted her up. As was usual when she felt happy, verses danced inside her. She could hear them while the old farmer, silent and ill at ease, let his animal trot along at an easy pace.

> Abstract mornings, chemistry, presence in the stone,
> Sun-kissed bounds of the source of light,
> Thrice-holy rhythms, powers! May my desires
> Melt in fiery flames into your slow becomings.
>
> Breath of my love, difficult intuition
> Of divine symbols joined to the centers of touch,
> Be the bond stretched from the loved one to her love,
> Secret revealed, dreams of eternity.

These contacts with nature provided a new and unanticipated experience while restoring vital contact with a universe she had completely forgotten. Obligations toward God were for her indistinguishable from social duty, the guide and driving force of action. To care for physical suffering, to ease moral suffering, to give in all circumstances preference to work, to duty, and to the mission to mankind, without worrying about other things or people, this had been the narrow path of her conduct. Brought into unexpected contact with this strange life, she now looked forward to she knew not what revelation to define more clearly the reality of man, ending this sense of superiority and isolation.

No direct message rose from the earth. Its beauty was spontaneously apparent, but Sister Lucinie had to reflect in order to remind herself that the same material elements in different combinations formed the entire world, and that man was remarkably like the rest of the universe. This reflection was based entirely on her previous knowledge. She sought, nevertheless, a more direct and intuitive lesson, a communication between the earth and herself.

When this anticipation remained unrealized, doubt formed inside her. She became afraid that she might confuse God's real action with her own desire to know Him. So long as this danger was present in her mind, her fear protected her against yielding easily, but from the time that her revelation had begun to act gently, she dreaded the possibility that she might discover a divine message or place where the only ruling force would be her human need to rejoin the all-powerful.

Everything became a symbol, everything became a sign, everything took on a private meaning. She dared neither refuse nor accept this insight into the material world, fearing that either decision would mean a betrayal of the truth.

She knew what she was looking or waiting for. It was neither a chemical or biological analogy, nor yet an ordinary method of self-expression, but a likeness of the soul. She believed in man's duality, conscious of the distinction and importance of soul and of body. She knew that to a certain extent the one was dependent on the other. The soul, for example, could order the body to fast but could not prevent it wasting away. The flesh might drag the soul with it into the sewer but still could exercise no influence on the logic of the mind. She knew that apart from their influence on each other they both were subject to influence from outside objects, often without being able to measure the extent of such influence. There was the further fact that the human soul expressed itself through the body and was difficult to define other than in relation to it.

Sister Lucinie expected to find a like duality in nature. She was looking for a spiritual brotherhood between the world and humanity, and although she had not yet clearly established this relationship, she had begun to downgrade man's importance. She was not thinking of denying him all mastery over the animal kingdom. To live, he had to eat, but this signified merely a momentary exchange of form, the transformation of one life into another without any real intervention of death. The plant and the stone were accordingly taking on for her an intrinsic value, which made them her companions.

This, however, was not enough. Notwithstanding her lack of confidence in herself, Sister Lucinie hoped for a more precise light. She had in her possession a sign that by its fulfillment or its failure might affirm or deny God's real presence within her and authorize her to shake off her doubts. She knew about this sign since the morning and because of it had refused the replacement for which Sister Perpétue had been so eager. It was an indication that promised her certainty within a relatively short interval.

Her most recent assignment was a mild case of whooping cough, complicated only by the number of her patients, who were three young boys. It was a daily pleasure to see their little round faces and to curl their silk-soft hair with her fingers when washing them. She was, however, not thinking of them. Their mother, Madame Senlis, was the sole cause of her concern.

Sister Lucinie had known her previously, having met her on the stairs in an apartment building where she happened to be working. Although their exchanges had been confined to a daily greeting, she had been well impressed by the woman's pleasant attitude and the way she carried herself. Now she was profoundly changed, living on her parents' farm, spiritless, letting her mother look after the children, slopping around in dressing gown and slippers under the weight of a still-invisible load, overcome by despair. This morning, Sister Lucinie had tried to make her fight her sluggishness, getting her out of bed early and helping her with her toilet. She had even enjoyed putting on the woman's make-up, for she hoped by bringing her back to her former interests to take her out of herself and dispel her gloom.

Amused, Madame Senlis joined in the play, while the nun explained to her casually:

"Christ urged His disciples to hide the marks of their fasting under feast-day clothes and perfume, and St. Francis de Sales told married women not to offend by their appearance either the wisdom of the old or the high spirits of the young."

She looked at the sick woman in the filtered light of the room, noting the bright color of the dress, the sparkling reflections of the hair, the pale face. Without warning, the forehead seemed to dry up, and while the nun tried to follow this transformation down the cheeks, she suddenly saw in front of her only a yellowish skeleton, a fleshless skull with three gold teeth shining in its mouth cavity.

Sister Lucinie looked away, but an irresistible force turned her face back toward the skull. "You are perfect," she said in a low tone. She raised her hand and followed the outline that God had sketched, sliding a finger the length of the jawbone in spite of her horror at the touch.

Why had she not then revealed what her soul had seen? Why had she not warned her: "Madame, God is going to take you. You know His goodness, His wisdom, His inspiration." Why, since this force penetrated and thickened the atmosphere with a crushing weight, did she not communicate her own distress instead of repeating mentally: "Don't be afraid. He can only love you."

In the obscure and painful duality of her love for God and her experience she prayed: "Attack only me. Let me undergo this trial by myself, and if she must die, then let Madame Senlis pass gently into eternity like a snowflake in a peaceful sky."

The hands in which the nun had buried her face slowly withdrew, but God remained silent, waiting. She felt that His will requested her approval, and a sudden revolt threw her back in a protective outburst toward the young mother. She had to keep her alive. It was her job to fight death, but nevertheless she paused almost as soon as she had made her foolish gesture. The realization of her helplessness crushed her, and the humble and habitual "Thy will be done" escaped from her lips in a sigh in the same moment in which the divine presence dispelled itself.

Indignation began again to mount inside her, but a subtle, pacifying doubt quickly replaced it. Madeleine Senlis, very much alive, was fastening big coral earrings in her ear lobes and smiling to her through those half-open red lips that revealed rows of shining teeth. That afternoon in the chapel the memory of the vision upset the nun once more. She censured her acceptance as a failure in her duty as a nurse and in her love for her neighbor, as well as a weakness that inevitably compelled, because of the equality of misfortune against which she no longer wanted to protect herself, her total acceptance of the divine will directed against herself. Nevertheless, in spite of her remorse and the anxiety caused by her acquiescence, she could not keep herself from reading into the occurrence a promise of prompt clarification of her own situation.

Chapter XIII

IT WAS TWILIGHT, the monotonous hour of the trip back in the high cart with Madame Senlis's father, of prayers interrupted by jokes, of a journey through the fields with their stiff stubble and the vineyards with their striking and vivid hues. This afternoon the farmer stopped unexpectedly before a row of vines that fell away toward the horizon hidden among the hills. To her astonishment, Sister Lucinie found herself with the reins in her hand, distracted from her meditation, while the man grabbed a basket and plunged among the laden vine branches spread out on the ground.

The old farmer lifted the leafy boughs heavy with grapes. Under his searching fingers the branches bent, trembled, lifted themselves, and suddenly grew proud in a movement of indescribable happiness, revealing to the watching nun joy in its most elemental form. The world revealed its essence and surrendered itself suddenly in an act of communion, a diffuse yet unique communion that rumbled around the man, took possession of the entire vine, then calmed itself after the first wave into a gentle and thrilling caress, while the blue-purple grapes piled up in the big basket.

The nun did not partake of this universal joy. She viewed it from without. The silence returned at times but was dominated by the vineyard so that its song without words or music and its living rhythm continued against a background of chirping cicadas. The intensity that at first had hurt the young woman by its total rejection of limits, its desire to be completely what it was, and its unexpected revelation of its existence, inspired in her a fierce enthusiasm as a spectator. In its presence she did not reflect whether she should accept or reject the joy, or if this transport of nature dominated by sense impressions clashed with her desire to refuse every material help in love. She joined in the lightsome happiness that imperceptibly became a spiritual action. The outside noise yielded in Sister Lucinie to a deep interior silence ready for the next call.

The weight of the farmer getting back into the cart broke the spell.

"That's good," he said. He looked from the overflowing basket to the vineyard. "I broke the ground and dug it," he went on. "For five months with five teams and a hundred men I carted off the stones and cleared the ground."

Sister Lucinie heard this voice that drowned out the

other voice of the festival, but her eyes and her mind remained on the vine that was now stirring all its leaves, welcoming the sun, reflecting the light and absorbing it into its fragile, transparent surfaces.

"People say," the farmer explained, "that man disfigures nature. As far as I am concerned, nothing exceeds the beauty of a well-worked plot of land, the splendor of a well-pruned vine, the sparkle of the green crops, or their almost crackling stillness when they are ripe. Nothing equals the purity of work when the dull, hard earth is cut by furrows of a deeper red or a darker violet, straight and crumbling, where the foot sinks and the grass dries out. Through this work I approach man and God, for without bread there is neither body nor soul."

His hard, firm outline became softer as she looked at him. He saw not the road but the fields, all the fields of the world, immense furrows stretching away to infinity. He had mentioned God as a matter of courtesy, merely using another word to express his own agreement with nature. He thought of himself as a worker, not a subordinate. This was his faith, his prayer, his communion, to participate on the material level in the work of the physical world, to neglect the spirit in order to reach the spirit, for, as he said, without the body as a springboard the soul cannot take flight. He had never known other scourgings than those of toil, other morning prayers than the rations to be distributed to his animals before dawn, other fastings than those imposed on him in his youth by a hunger that was always sharpened and seldom long satisfied, other moral code than that of uprightness and perfection in his work. All his harshness toward others derived from an inflexible severity toward himself, his eagerness for work, his perpetual response, and his productive power.

Sister Lucinie studied him with admiration. He went ahead with the certainty that comes from doing one's job, and he countered moral and religious scruples with the beauty and fruitfulness of the task itself. And recalling the celebration of a moment ago, the rejoicing of plant life in which God had revealed Himself, the nun thought that this man was definitely not deceived. The intense practice of a major virtue sufficed for salvation, and defects were wiped out in the presence of achievement. A man, his action, and his soul should not remain independent of their results, and the final verdict depended on both the one and the other. Compared with this visible and measurable work, what did Sister Lucinie contribute? What net sum of cares, consolations, and prayers could she offer? Without always observing her monastic rule scrupulously she had known fatigue, anxiety, disappointments, and joys. She had swept houses and cleaned wounds, consoled the sad, restored courage, always on the border of matter and spirit; and without the spirit perhaps there would have been in all this neither satisfaction of the body nor a body itself.

Before God she could present her work perhaps as well done as it was permitted her to do. She brought to it, quite apart from the notion of salvation, a desire of perfection equal to that of this man, and she added this love of others of which he seemed to be unaware. He did not hate his neighbor and remained open to pity and friend-

123

ship, but love of the soil and of work triumphed, while in her love of her neighbor took the upper hand.

Before God, nevertheless, both of them might be right, in so far as both had served mankind with all their strength and forgetting themselves.

Chapter XIV

SISTER LUCINIE sat under the big pear tree on
the edge of a plot of alfalfa. Each day she passed the
siesta hour in the garden full of roses, fruits, and corn-
stalks, and cut by silent canals.

The heat of the sun combined with weariness to crush
the nun as she said her rosary in a mood of depression.
She finished a decade and thought that she was nearing
the end of the month of August and of her stay in this
place. The children were better and in a few days would
go off to vacation with their Aunt Geneviève. Not only
was there no longer anything to keep her here, but she
knew that her presence was distasteful to Madeleine
Senlis's older sister who had arrived the previous evening
and who — like everyone else in the family — felt that

the young mother should have been able by herself to look after her children.

The nun was due to come for the last time tomorrow and accordingly had now only a few hours to help the young woman or prepare her for approaching death, but she felt herself utterly unequipped for this task. In three weeks she had raised her from her apathy, restoring her taste for beauty and society, yet had scarcely mentioned religion for fear of reviving Madame Senlis's depression.

She also questioned her own interpretation of the divine warning, wondering as she looked at Madeleine's still far from complete restoration if she should not read into it not a sign of death but rather a symbol of the instability of the living body, of this painted and fastidious face.

She hesitated between the flesh and the spirit, uncertain which had first call on her attention, for the secrets the sick woman had confided to her, while revealing a hidden sorrow, gave no indication of grave sin. She was in the presence of a somewhat frivolous soul. It lacked depth or great wisdom, but it was exceedingly pure. The entire drama of her life resulted from her husband's vices and from his disregard for her need of integrity and conjugal innocence. The presence of a corrupted man had taken away even her will to live, notwithstanding the love she retained for him. Without really understanding the situation too clearly, she in fact wanted to die to free herself from this wickedness, but also to give him the chance of a happiness which he no longer found with her.

The woman's longing for purity troubled Sister Lucinie. She understood that she thought very little

126

about those virtues for which others struggled desperately. She went through life as though lacking one half of her humanity, concentrated on God and on her interior need for charity and compassion. Her freedom from most of the difficulties encountered by others built a fence of calm around her, but she tended, in consequence, to doze off in her affection for God, to create around Him a veil of vagueness. In her affectionate and fearful way she loved something she did not know.

But the harsh impact she had experienced just a few months earlier, the discovery of the passions that had sprung up around her, had bewildered her. She knew previously that such passions existed, having often met them in her earlier work as a nurse. But it was only now that she had wakened from her sleep and her unquestioning assumptions. For some days she had succeeded in suppressing her fear, or at least her refusal of the divine, by the sense of guilt resulting from her acceptance of the death of Madame Senlis. Today this no longer sufficed. She had to prepare the woman, for she was finally convinced that she was going to die, yet she did not know what she should tell her. She was torn between a desire to spare her unnecessary suffering and a need to ensure that she did not arrive unprepared before the last judge.

For a full two weeks she had postponed action from day to day, searching in vain for an adequate explanation, for the right words that never came. Even her Christian outlook seemed to have left her. For the first time good and evil did not seem to exist as absolutes, but only in relation to a circle of persons and circumstances. She had the impression that God stayed outside every judgment, leaving to those who performed an action the duty of deciding its true value. To condemn or to absolve was a function of each one's own conscience.

She raised her eyes. Madame Senlis was standing in front of her, bending down in her flowered dress to lie on the waving alfalfa.

"Now," Sister Lucinie told herself, "now I must speak to her. I'll never again get such an opportunity."

Nevertheless, she remained silent, and it was the newcomer who expressed a similar interior distress, holding out her emaciated hands through which one could see the reddish sunlight.

"Do you believe," she asked, "that God is good? What I mean is, do you believe that He can take pity on a soul, lift it out of its sins, and draw it toward Himself? Do you not rather think that logic demands that His laws should be applied with objective indifference, that they are Himself, so that His will doesn't enter into the matter? That when the Lord's mills have ground the wheat, His screen lets the flour pass through and rejects the bran?"

"I believe" — Sister Lucinie's voice changed its tone, becoming impersonal, as if she were reading sentences from a book that expressed a thought other than her own — "I believe that the terms of death and birth are unsatisfactory. There does not exist one life or two lives, but an eternal life that changes and undergoes evolutions. In the same way as there is not an absolutely fixed body, but rather short-lived and changing forms eternally in movement, so also there is no such thing as dissimilar and impenetrable souls. Your soul is not all light. It also has shadows, which depend on a body so subject to

128

transformation that it will cease to sustain the soul in a common reality, like it now is."

The two fell silent. The nun was conscious of a return of her concern, because her words did not reflect what her thought had been before she had spoken or what she now believed on this subject.

She looked at Madame Senlis and saw once again the marks of death, not exactly the fleshless skull of the other day, but the irregular lines hollowed out on the temple, the sunken eyeballs, and the protruding jawbones.

The farm awoke slowly. The noise of the mules stamping in the courtyard was mixed with the orders given by the men and the tinkling of a piano. Madame Senlis checked Sister Lucinie's movement.

"Stay where you are," she urged her. "Geneviève is going to play, and if the children wake up, she will look after them."

The player struck a chord, then another, hesitated, searched for the right notes, then struck up a waltz. The nun listened. The music astonished her because it had a lightness and a rhythm of which she had never thought the player capable. In her mind she saw her in the dining room with its brick paving and half-opened shutters. The room was filled with light. The brown floor tiles gradually grew and became large squares of marble under the feet of the nun, now only a silhouette in her ill-defined gown that opened out into a wide collar. All her cares faded away and her soul shot upward with no form other than that of this dance and no scenery other than the giddily steep floor on which spun an aerial double, a tenuous body whose feelings repeated themselves in her. All of this fairylike whiteness, this spotless floor, this lily-white gown, these acacia flowers now falling slowly in unsubstantial bunches, billowed about her like a great feast, outstripped the music, lingered in silence, and with gentle throbbings vanished among the nun's black robes.

Madeleine Senlis had fallen asleep. The bewildered nun still held in her mind the last crumbs of this unheard-of evasion, of this lapse of her whole self into a worldly pleasure. Her reason had neither participated in nor consented to the unanticipated fault, which no warning temptation had preceded. But did it constitute a sin? The Church forbade not the movement of the dance but the contact with one's partner and the intoxication of the senses. Sister Lucinie had experienced neither element. She had been the very essence of the waltz freed from all bodily attachment, a light, an attitude, rather than a sensation. The fault, if there was one, consisted in the intensity of her contemplation that gave her a power she was beginning no longer to control. The concentration of her mind was now taking her inside matter, as had happened with the wild swaying of the vines or this lone waltz.

Such inability to control her sensations did not, however, seem to involve sin. God was according her an intimate experience of the elements, even when they expressed themselves under an intangible form like music. Whether translated by her body or imagination, the impression lacked intrinsic value. What was important was to reveal this current of impetuous love, the force and universality of which she was beginning to understand, a love that joined the dance to the vineyard, to man and to God. This love resulted not only from a separate body or from a soul, but even from the molecule within the body.

Sister Lucinie felt her heart expand. A corner of the veil had been raised and she waited for what was to follow, dazzled by this first light which nevertheless revealed only light itself to her and clarified nothing else. She stretched out her hand in the grass, and this involuntary movement brought her halfway back to her distress. She touched Madame Senlis. She desired deeply to exchange her knowledge with the sleeping woman. She felt that, relaxed like a child, she was still suffering. In her mind she embraced her and raised her toward that great brightness, while her affection for the frail mother dissolved in the eternal love. Time seemed to stand still.

After a while the eyes reopened. For the entire afternoon the calm of their communion remained, long after they had left the garden to go back to their accustomed tasks. But they did not express their peace in words, both of them remaining in the uncertainty of their mental message. Sister Lucinie had the feeling of being merely a link between God and Madeleine, something like a tube in a radio receiver.

Chapter XV

‘‘W H A T do you think of my sister?’’ Geneviève asked.

The cart was carrying the two women to town, and Madame Tibout drove the horse with a firm hand. Sister Lucinie looked at the vines which today were silent, crushed by the relentless heat of ground and air. She feared to give an answer that might hurt Madame Senlis or arouse her companion's suspicions.

"I find her tired." She watched Geneviève's reactions without looking at her, pretending to be absorbed in the movement of the reins. "Very tired," she added.

Geneviève recalled her younger sister's face. She could not see the depth of her sickness under the cream, make-up, and powder. Nevertheless, Madeleine's frail appearance, her body much too thin for a pregnant woman, and her excessive sensitivity disturbed her deeply. Recalling her mother's letter asking her to come, she was astonished at its total lack of understanding of and pity for the feebleness of her younger sister. Affection coupled with alarm began to revive within her.

"From a medical point of view," said Sister Lucinie, "your sister needs more attention. At the beginning I thought she was under a doctor's care, but I was wrong." The nun recognized the good points in this despotic and tender Geneviève. "I have nothing definite to go on," she continued, "but I think you should watch her heart. It doesn't seem to me natural for a young woman to be so depressed."

"Mama mentioned it in her letter, but do you really believe it?" Geneviève studied Sister Lucinie, who merely raised her hand in an equivocal gesture.

"I cannot be categorical, but undoubtedly character changes may result from physiological causes. Besides, your sister suffers greatly from her conjugal disappointments."

She paused, not knowing just how far she could go without hurting or betraying Madame Senlis. Then she recognized that the effort was quite hopeless, and that only her duty as a nurse forced her to make it. Her arguments became hesitant, and even her voice ceased to convince, because her faith unbalanced her request, not her clearly known and acknowledged official faith, but an uncontrollable and unknowable submission that rose out of the deepest depths of her being. The religious drama was now being enacted in the subliminal regions of her soul.

The duality of her attitude came also from her compassion. She wanted to warn the others of the possibly imminent departure, to prepare them and thus prevent an emotional and dangerous surprise.

Geneviève continued to guide the animal, but deep in thought she pulled unthinkingly on the bridle, so that the horse stopped just where the path met the road.

"This child," she sighed, "I'd give my life for her. I'd help her in any circumstances, and then she leaves me on the outside, refusing to share her sufferings with me, her joys or her life."

"She loves you," Sister Lucinie said. "But she lacks aggressiveness. She fights in her own way, maintaining her privacy and letting nobody get mixed up in her problems."

"So what about you?"

All of Geneviève's motherly jealously was expressed in the question, in the pained tone of her voice, and in the eyes that avoided those of the nun so as not to expose their anger.

"You stand for the severity of a mother with all that this implies in terms of probable scoldings, intervention between husband and wife, and imposition of a line of conduct. As for me, I am just someone in whom she can confide, and the facts were told to me only in general terms and never in detail. My function is simply to relieve the pain. I have no right to give advice. I am an equal who can be quickly dropped from the scene without causing complications. All I do is to console."

"There must be something more," Madame Tibout insisted. "Just now her expression was overflowing with confidence and friendship. I shall never forget it."

Touching the reins, she put the horse in motion again.

134

Her jealousy was smothering her concern, and this, in turn, was hiding from her the really important aspect of the matter: Madeleine's dangerous condition. Sister Lucinie tried to bring the discussion back to its original object.

"I was the first to believe in her exhaustion and in her illness. Your mother . . . "

"My mother," Geneviève interrupted in a harsh voice, "does not know what pity is. Life was very hard on her: fifteen children, ten of them living, crushing work on the farm, never a break, never a trip. She considers that she has done enough work and does not want to be burdened with any further responsibility. I can understand her point of view, but it has been hard for the children."

"I pass no judgment on her," Sister Lucinie replied. These digressions upset her, because they were getting close to town. It was already in sight, spread out, white, dry, despite the trees on the sidewalks and along the winding river with its marshy curves. "I merely want to explain that she is mistaken when she thinks this suffering is caused by a woman's imagination. I believe there is a deeper ailment."

"Deeper," Geneviève repeated, turning the thought over in her mind for a moment as the carriage bumped along the rough border of the road.

Sister Lucinie was not pleased by this sluggishness of understanding, the lack of normal reactions, the depression of the older woman in her anger and jealousy. Suddenly, as if the threat enclosed in the phrase was directed at her alone, Madame Tibout regained her strength.

"What symptoms make you say that?" she asked.

Her demanding voice had become hostile. Sister

Lucinie was sickened by the sentimental selfishness, the need to be self-assertive and dictatorial, which possibly had led to the younger sister's spiritual solitude.

"From the medical viewpoint," she answered dryly, "the excessive weakness, inertia, indifference, and especially the loss of weight, seem to me to constitute sufficient alarm signals. Now as a nurse accustomed to the reactions of the sick, I can tell you one thing without hesitation — your sister is lost."

"What are you saying?"

Geneviève was stunned. The shock of this straightforward declaration so upset her that she lost her self-confidence and condescension.

"I say what I say," the nun insisted as she stepped down from the cart outside the convent door. "Make whatever use you wish of my warning."

She felt herself alone in the struggle, and the entire family looked to her like a wall. All the anger of the nurse at this mass refusal to face facts sprang up inside her, just as it did every time she clashed with the indifference of those in good health toward the sick or the unbelief that called into question the reality of pain or the value of treatment. But her anger on this occasion was sterile. She knew the destined fate of Madame Senlis and realized that no effort could alter it, and still she persisted against God.

She went into the house. There was nobody home, not even Sister Anne of the Cross, so she had to start the supper and lay the table while waiting for the others, even though what she wanted with all her soul was the peace of the chapel and the support of her sisters. She had feared God's visit, but He had taken pity on her when He heard her admission: "Forgive me, Lord. I do not have the strength to follow you. I don't know the secret of your wisdom, but I am terrified by this death which comes to all."

Nevertheless, in her sorrow this death she had feared suddenly appeared as a haven of peace, an end to uncertainty, a landing place. It was like a night's sleep, less terrifying than the blind task that she undertook day after day without attempting to define her aims. For her vocation was to bring man across this unknown space filled with promises, while her profession held him on the slope, delaying the call for a little while.

Chapter XVI

CAPTAIN SENLIS got to his feet. He was amused and touched by this dress of his wife's that he had forgotten, this pale blue satin already out of style but so pliant and brilliant that it created a sense of joy. He took Madeleine in his arms, but touching only her back so as not to disturb her dress. The young woman felt at peace again. This tribute filled her with happiness and put her sad memories to flight. It seemed to her that everything could start all over, that she had exaggerated her husband's conduct. Seeing herself as a queen, she foresaw a brighter future, and with a light touch of her fingers on his hair she forgave everything. He understood the reconciliation, drew her closer to him, ready to swing her around the table in one of those wild dances in which he worked off his surplus vitality. But the door opened and the three children appeared followed by Sister Lucinie, to take their places at the table.

"Sister," Madeleine asked, "how do I look?"

She stood smiling under the light, and the nun studied her from head to foot, her eyes raising themselves slowly again to rest on her face.

"Very good," she said; "but open your eyes."

"They are open," the young woman exclaimed, laughing.

The captain looked at this tall black-and-white form, upright in the shade, and recalled who she was. This was the nun for whom he had opened the door at Madame Vedrine's, and the memory disturbed him. But her present attitude raised a more serious, indefinable, yet unbearable fear. Madeleine came toward him, leading the nun by the hand.

"You have no idea, Francis, of the condition from which she has restored me. I no longer believed in anything, and now I begin to live again."

All his concern disappeared as Captain Senlis heard his wife's words. Sister Lucinie became more human and Madeleine more vivacious. The best thing was to postpone his empty apprehensions until the doctor came. The nurse was responsible for these doubts and suspicions. She had a melancholy air even when she smiled. This was her last evening, and soon the house would be free from her troublesome presence. Nevertheless, he did not share Geneviève's annoyance, experiencing rather a sense of pleasure at the nurse's maternal attentiveness to Madeleine, and it amused him to see her sit beside her as a mother beside her favorite child.

The meal was eaten in a relaxed atmosphere. They all had had a bad night but gradually they were shaking off their fears. Only Sister Lucinie did not speak, but then she seldom did, and her presence cast no shadow over the gaiety at the table encouraged by the aroma of the food and the sparkling of the wines as the light rested on them in shimmering gold.

Sister Lucinie served each with a fragrant cup of coffee and let the children run in the cool safety of the corridor. She could not make up her mind to leave this happy circle. She saw this resurrection without being able to believe in it, just as she had not been entirely able to believe in the death of Madame Senlis. She lingered in their company, hearing in spite of herself a conversation she had no right to understand, feeling that she was doing wrong, yet unable to resolve to leave.

Then Madame Senlis stood up, made a gesture toward the window, and collapsed in the arms of Sister Lucinie, who happened to be the closest and most attentive, though she did not know what to do with this dead thing, as light as a child, whom the others were shaking.

"The children," she said, "get the children out of the passage. We must put her to bed."

Geneviève went out.

"You," she ordered Francis, "get a doctor straight away."

Madame Senlis's old parents followed her into the room. She laid the body, the arms hanging down lifeless, on the bed, took off the satin dress and the shoes with the pointed toes, and tried unsuccessfully to massage her. She knew there was nothing she could do, that Madeleine was already on her way to God, and that she had not received the Last Sacraments. But all of this took second place, and she continued her duty as a nurse. The doctor, after a long wait, interrupted her task. What difference did it now make that this heart had been worn out for quite a time, that nobody had worried about the frail wife, that she herself had been so weary and sick of living that she had avoided attention?

Perhaps she already knew the reality of the message received under the shade of the pear tree. She brought it with her where she was going as she also brought the glory of this last day, the joy of the meal, the final understanding with her husband, the success of her blue gown. While Madeleine lay there in another dress which Francis had put on her, Sister Lucinie took a last look at the bony outlines of her cheeks and the deep-seated eyes she had been watching while they ate. Even in death she remained beautiful, a fresh face in which the half-closed eyes revealed two dark eyeballs, a shining head of curly hair which her husband smoothed down with gentle touches. Around her were her sorrowing family, and the mother who choked down a sob that never quite escaped.

When Sister Lucinie left the farm that evening for the last time, a distant storm announced its approach in the dark masses of the clouds. Madame Senlis's old father urged on his horse which trotted along in the wind and the dust, while in the fields great eddies of clods, straw, and twigs swept around, to envelop the flocks of sheep in their whirling course and disappear without warning.

"The rain is going to catch us," the old man growled.

He felt miserable and ashamed beside the nun, and he wanted to accuse himself and excuse himself at the same

141

time. But he said nothing more. He lifted his face toward the horizon, aware of Sister Lucinie's submission and her fear expressed in prayers which he did not understand but which he recognized by the movement of her lips. The thunder crashed now with the sounds of falling trees, of rumblings endlessly repeated from the clouds, and of flashes that lighted up the carriage in their menacing glare.

Sister Lucinie looked at the dark sky, listening to the noise. Their path through the storm seemed endless, an evidence of the divine anger. The old man seemed to share her thought, for he said to himself: "It's going to rain and she will be cold."

The first drops began to fall, then the hailstones rattled, small but abundant, spreading a snowlike blanket on the tarred surface of the road. The horse went on with sudden bursts of speed and unexpected lunges, his nostrils open, ear trembling and straight back.

The man was crying under the flood of rain that soaked them and softened Sister Lucinie's stiff cornette. The nun, worn out by the noise, the lightning flashes, and their dangerous journey, placed a compassionate hand on the knotty, sunburned, earth-browned fingers that held the reins.

"You couldn't help it," she shouted into the wind. "She was too sick."

He continued to cry, ignoring the words that she hurled at him through the storm and which the thunderclaps allowed him only to half-hear, but he was thinking that she had helped and consoled his child, that she had held her for the last time in her arms, that she was like an inspired person in the fury of the elements, and he

142

loved her. They reached the end of the storm just as night fell. Sister Lucinie, trembling, climbed down from the carriage. He turned his horse and urged it homeward while she went toward the door.

She opened it. The night light in the hall was just bright enough to outline the warm passage. The noise of the voices she loved reached her from the refectory. Sister Perpétue would probably be the first to come, to make a fuss, and to bring her to her room. She heard steps. She lifted her heavy head and recognized Sister Dominique, then, still more surprising and more protective, Mother Cécile, the old Superior and Novice Mistress at the motherhouse, appeared. Sister Lucinie smiled toward the outstretched arms and the forms that grew in number, almost indistinguishable, for all she could see were the eyes for which she had been looking.

"The poor child is at her last gasp," said the visitor, wiping away the water which was pouring down the bloodless face. "Sister Anne of the Cross, run and get her some herb tea. Sister Dominique, let's go and change her clothes."

The cell seemed too small to hold more than three persons, but God also came. Sister Lucinie, crushed under the too great weight, swooned away.

Chapter XVII

"I CANNOT DESCRIBE all that to you without a sense of shame," Sister Lucinie said. "It seems to me that by disclosing God's gifts to me I betray His confidence. Were it not for the rule and your questioning, I should never have mentioned any part of it."

The two of them were again together the day following the storm, the old Superior skilled in scrutinizing the consciences of her nuns, and the distressed sister. The confession she had just made, the sense of protection provided by the room, the distant sounds of the other nuns working about the house, all these things deprived the young sister of every wish to act, to defend herself, to humiliate herself, even to want to live. Now Mother Cécile knew and would take full charge.

Perhaps the Visitatrix to the overseas houses of the Order would take her back to France with her or isolate her from the others as a dangerous person. Sister Lucinie experienced no reaction when she contemplated either possibility. Feeling beyond the reach of any blow, she closed her eyes, sank down into Sister Dominique's armchair, and fell asleep.

When she woke up, Mother Cécile spoke to her as though she had never dozed off, and Sister Lucinie understood that the interval of sleep must have been very short. Nevertheless, it had sufficed to overcome her drowsiness and momentary indifference. She saw herself once more in the presence of a judge. The old Superior did not indeed seem to be a very terrifying judge. Sitting upright in her chair, her eyes half-closed, she was simply a gentle and calm old woman, but Sister Lucinie knew that her questions were capable of boring down into the depths of the soul, and that the test she had just been through had completely bared her thoughts. She had no idea what would follow. She hoped in a general way that her former Novice Mistress and Superior would destroy this force within her and restore the kind of intellectual fatigue that results from overexertion, and still she knew that nothing could change her. Her experience would prevail against all the arguments of the Reverend Mother and she would defend that experience in order to remain faithful to God.

"What representation of the Lord do you worship?" the Superior asked. "Do you prefer to speak to one in particular of the three persons of the Trinity?"

The question jarred Sister Lucinie. Her questioner was going to force her to define positions that she had

145

adopted without reflection, and she feared that she would not be able to remember clearly enough to answer without making a mistake.

"That depends on the circumstances and on the prayers I happen to be saying," she answered slowly. "In general, when I am not using formulas fixed by usage, but my own words, I speak to God without attributing to Him a specific form."

She paused for a reaction. The old Superior's face was attentive but blank, providing no guidance. She continued.

"When I try to see God, I always select a Gospel scene. I come back inevitably to Jesus."

"Do you find it easy to obtain mental images?"

"No," Sister Lucinie confessed. "I build with words. I form a spoken text inside me, and sometimes in a flash I gain a quick outline without seeing anything firmly. I grasp a detail — a smile, a glance, a gesture, an expression, the thing that happens to be precisely the most vulnerable in a person, and then I always forget it. What I mean is that it never remains with me. It will not come back later if I want it."

"When you think of another person, of me, for example," Mother Cécile asked, "do you see me?"

The younger woman again leaned her head against the chair arm. She never could control her memories, and consequently she preferred to answer after a quick test. She thought in turn of Sister St. Jean, of the pastor, of little Jacques Senlis, of Mother Cécile herself, without looking at her, then she put her hands over her eyes to plunge herself into total darkness.

"No," she explained, "I do not see you, not even in a

hazy or fugitive way. Nevertheless, without describing you as I do with Jesus, without constructing you in any way, I know how you are made, my mind recalls you."

The old Superior was not fully satisfied.

"This memory, does it come from a calculated observation, or does it rather form itself without an act of the will?"

Sister Lucinie reflected again. The mechanism of her thought processes escaped her, and she did not believe that she could answer more specifically without further study and meditation. Nevertheless, she searched her mind and expressed her vague ideas.

"I don't think I examined you to fix your characteristics, except of course the very first time, but I was so excited then that I noticed nothing clearly. My image of you was formed during my noviceship, when I saw you very frequently."

"You say 'your image,'" the older woman commented.

"That's not the right word," Sister Lucinie answered. "I don't know the exact shape of your mouth. And yet I do," she corrected herself, looking downward so as not to see her questioner. "I know that it is full-lipped and rather large, and those are characteristics I have observed. I recall the detail because it struck me, but as a matter of fact I think rather of your different expressions. When you smile, when you are annoyed, when you are attentive, your eyes change. When you are happy, for example."

She stopped speaking, because she was no longer thinking of the Reverend Mother's eyes, but of her puckered eyebrows, of the prominence of her cheekbones, of her crooked and placid smile.

147

"Ah," she sighed, "I know that within me there are many images of you, but I cannot see them. They are at the back of my eyes and thanks to them I can define the details, but I do not see them. Besides, I can scarcely assemble these fragments into a whole. Rather, I am able to convey the impression they give me, which is that your joy is good."

"I understand," Mother Cécile agreed, and Sister Lucinie thought that she was generous to say so, for the images which she imagined she stored behind her eyes, deep in her mind, were quite inadequate to express these stealthy sensations to which she appealed to refresh her memory. Nevertheless, the extreme precision of her memories did not reflect the vagueness of their sources.

"I realize," she said, "that without intending to I try to resemble those whose image I seek to recall. Just now I was talking about your eyes but I was not looking at them in my mind. Rather, in spite of myself, I was puckering my eyebrows exactly as you do."

The Superior followed this analysis, mentally noting its precision. This quality gave at least a strong indication that she was not dealing with a case of blind self-deception.

"Do you think of God in exactly the same way when you pray or when you meditate?"

She wanted at all costs to prevent Sister Lucinie from engaging in a false adventure. She loved her, but she loved in her the strong woman, the devoted nun endowed with sensitivity that almost enabled her to read the minds of those around her. These qualities had ceased to be visible yesterday, on her arrival, in the girl soaked by

148

the storm, neither did they show this morning during the long confession full of hesitancies. But now she saw them manifest themselves once more, as soon as she placed her on a ground where she was more sure of herself.

"To be exact, I think very rarely of God, if by that you mean that I attempt to determine what He is like in a personal way. The sense of my helplessness as compared with the intelligence of the Church, the pleasure of taking advantage of a fully-fashioned concept, the certain knowledge that all the major problems have been definitively solved remove any temptation I might have to try to think them out again. Of course I think of Him, but I appreciate Him in terms of what you taught us. Or at least that was true in the past," she added, "for more recently I have been trying to force myself to search for Him again. Up to two months ago I lost myself in God but without fathoming His depths."

"And at that time, what was your prevailing sensation?"

"Oh," Sister Lucinie cried in an outburst of love, "I believed in His goodness, in the certainty of His love and of His pardon. I always found God of the Sermon on the Mount."

"You mean to say you found Christ?"

"No, God, just God."

"But," Mother Cécile intervened in a gentle voice, "God did not appear in the Sermon on the Mount. What you find there is Christ defining the proper way to behave."

"Do you think so?" Sister Lucinie took a moment to go

over the Gospel passage in her mind. "Yes," she agreed humbly, "I saw Him as someone good and gentle, because that is what He told us we should be."

"Nevertheless, when God appeared to Moses on Mount Sinai, was He not the awful God of anger?"

Sister Lucinie remained silent. She knew that she could not hold her own in a discussion with Mother Cécile, because all her viewpoints were conditioned by a sense of hesitancy and diffidence. From the time of her noviceship she had lived in a closed world controlled by two or three ideas, a world from which she made no effort to escape, guiding her conduct and her attitudes by her ideals of pardon, love, and charity. The Superior might take her on a voyage through the Bible in search of a warrior God, but all that she would be able to see would be the unfathomable divine forgiveness for a primitive people, and in the outline of God provided in Exodus, nothing more than a human representation similar to that which simple peoples were able to sketch for themselves through the narratives of the prophets.

Sister Lucinie took only a moment to make all these thoughts clear in her mind, in the silence of the little room, but she was unwilling to share her point of view with the Superior, fearing that the result would be a direct attack on her dogmatic deviations.

Mother Cécile was trying to establish if the young nun was a victim of mysticism, not because she found it impossible to believe in direct communion between God and the creature, but because this experienced guide of souls had an innate distrust of all the deceptions and flights of imagination, both voluntary and involuntary, in which nervous women indulged.

The old Superior's last phrase had forced the young nun to analyze her intimate knowledge of God, not her intellectual appreciation, but the understanding derived from direct contact. What Mother Cécile wanted to know was whether the notion Sister Lucinie formed of God could arise automatically from her meditations on the Bible, or if on the contrary God made Himself felt without relation to any mental activity. The young woman understood exactly the point that interested her questioner, and that helped, for she herself also wanted to establish the truth, and this doubt which paralleled her own, this uneasy and questioning curiosity, clarified the debate by forcing her to probe depths which she normally avoided in her daily life, from lack of knowledge of how to probe them, from lack of time, and also from a vague fear that such probing might displease the Lord.

"I believe," she said, looking at Mother Cécile, who waited patiently for an answer, "that I express myself badly when I try to explain how God appears. I use the word 'force' and thereby suggest an idea of violence which in fact does not exist. A presence simply weighs upon me, a presence too powerful for my weakness. I yield because I resist, just as I would hurt myself if I pushed against that wall in an attempt to destroy it. I should merely bruise myself without achieving any result. If I let myself go freely to welcome my visitor, perhaps I should die as a result, but He would not do me any intended harm."

"What do you know about that?" the Superior demanded.

She avoided meeting Sister Lucinie's eye, bowing her

head in prayer. Her mind, nevertheless, was alert. She did not come into contact with the nuns too often, because her functions as a Visitatrix did not let her stay for any length of time in a convent in the overseas missions. She had a question in her mind about Sister Lucinie ever since the Mother General had praised the young nun in terms that were too laudatory for her taste. Although Mother Cécile believed in God, her faith was conditioned by a long experience of people that caused her to tend toward a materialism she herself did not suspect. Now, Mother General's favorable opinion was not based on specific facts, but rather on the atmosphere that Sister Lucinie spread around her: her attitude of prayer, the light in her eyes, her goodness, her intuition, the special sound of her voice, and of her singing.

She attached greater weight to the more prosaic and precise comments of Sister Dominique, Sister Anne of the Cross, or Sister St. Jean, than to Mother General's eulogies. She believed that the affectionate comments of the first two and the hostility of the third added up to a portrait of a nursing sister who had reached a high degree of perfection. The enthusiasm of the community Superior, no less than the reservations and accusations of Sister St. Jean, had prepared her for something of a dreamer, a suspicion confirmed by Mother St. Augustine's letter. Nevertheless, the young woman's manual skill and the extraordinary quantity of work she performed each day failed to match such a theory, and consequently she now found herself again in her presence without being able to make up her mind.

Sister Lucinie sat very upright in the armchair, almost motionless, her face half turned to the window. Her eyes followed the line of light between the closed ventilators and the wall or turned to study her companion, but when she spoke, her gaze seemed to penetrate the depths of her own soul or fly away toward an infinity that carried her far from her companion. Mother Cécile was conscious of these flights but she could not deny the physical attraction of the young woman. Sister Lucinie did not let herself get excited; on the contrary, she revealed a sweet and calm peace in her every feature. Even more, however, than this placid beauty, more than the seriousness and goodness of her mouth, the purity that shone from her face troubled the Visitatrix. She could not define the exact source of their serenity, whether the high forehead, the clean line of Sister Lucinie's oval face, or the remarkably pellucid gleam of her eyes. No doubt the impression was enhanced by the quiet bearing and the economy and precision of her gestures. But basically, she felt, it must have its source in her spirituality. When Sister Lucinie said that she enjoyed divine visions, there could be no question of deliberate deception. Nevertheless, even admitting this, there always remained the possibility of a mistake.

"This force was never violent," she said. "It comes, I experience it, but at the first movement of rejection it leaves."

"But why should you reject it?" Mother Cécile asked.

A vivid blush lighted the tilted face, spreading outward to lose itself under her headband. Sister Lucinie seemed suddenly very young. Even her lips grew softer and her face rounder as she answered:

"I'm afraid."

Then she became again the calm and self-possessed

woman the others knew. The emotion faded so fast that Mother Cécile could not determine the intensity or continuity of the sensation. All she knew about the nun was what she herself would or could say, and this excessive reserve annoyed her. She entered into this soul by the normal opening of obedience to the rule without being able to decide how much remained hidden, willingly or otherwise, without knowing if the agitation revealed a moment ago continued under the impassive mask, or if this outward appearance of calm correctly reflected an interior reality.

"Yes," Sister Lucinie went on, "I wanted to reach God, just as we all do, but I didn't expect to find Him under this form."

She was grateful to Mother Cécile for permitting these long intervals of silence. At the beginning she had felt a need for the Reverend Mother's extreme cleverness but she had also feared it. Now, after the earlier insistent questioning, she appreciated the value of the wordless pauses during which she could look inside herself. Without realizing it, however, she was using this device to escape the authority of her Superior. All she communicated to her as a result of her study of her soul was a stylized and precise pattern from which the uncertainty had been removed.

She did not understand why she had feared death, but this attitude resulted mainly from the fact that she no longer revolted emotionally when faced by it. The rapid, almost smiling, moment in Madame Senlis's home had wiped out her instinctive horror. Today she could contemplate the threat of death and believe herself almost ready to accept it. And since she analyzed only the present she was unable to rediscover the terror that she had expressed in her former answer. The happy surprise of this discovery created no intense joy. It resembled rather the flickering flame of a candle that has just been lighted and has not yet succeeded in establishing itself and piercing the darkness. She awaited a brighter fire, a mounting flame, the indescribable glow in the deepest recesses of her heart. While her soul thus prepared itself in complete silence, deliberately calming all feelings and reactions, and eliminating every thought, the forgotten and distant voice of the Superior came to her:

"Who tells you that this force is God?"

Mother Cécile was reaching the point of admitting the existence of this power, but she was not yet willing to recognize God in it. In her refusal to admit the strange or miraculous she saw no lack of faith. She trusted her own soul as a citadel of wisdom, and this nun who refused to look at her, whose gaze wandered off into unexplored regions, seemed now an unbalanced visionary, a threat to the peace of the convent and of the entire order. It was part of her task to impose uniformity, to watch over the general behavior of every convent, to prevent any deviation in conduct. Sister Lucinie shone too brightly for the normal gloom of daily life. She ought to bring her down to the common level of undistinguished virtue whose height and depth she determined by refusing to sanction either misconduct or mysticism.

Nevertheless, she wanted to give Sister Lucinie every opportunity to explain herself, because she esteemed the Mother General and had confidence in that lady's quite extraordinary wisdom, a wisdom based on intuition and profound goodness, not on logic and the rule like her own. Every novelty provoked Mother Cécile's suspicion. Instinctively her first approach to others was to look for the common human basis. Unconsciously she threw up a barrier of resistance against reactions she could not anticipate. By contrast, her successor as head of the order assumed in some, though of course not in all, cases the existence of spiritual greatness. Sister Lucinie, marked with this sign, raised a problem for Mother Cécile. But by a simultaneous though contrary reaction, the illogicality of which escaped her, she told herself that the serenity of the young woman, her coldness, the absence of the emotional excitement that she feared and sought to expose as a defect, denied the reality of a supernatural message. She knew to what extent the emotions of these nuns brought up in a hothouse atmosphere might go astray and get out of control, but she also had some idea how such an opportunity would fill her with uncontrollable joy. Sister Lucinie's calm reassured her as regards the future of the order and made her doubt her own judgment.

"Who told you that this force is God?" she said once again.

A scarcely perceptible change occurred in the young nun. She now looked at Mother Cécile, yet seemed to be listening to the noises outside, and she gripped the chair arms tightly in her clenched hands. Even her voice changed, losing the high tone that had annoyed Mother Cécile at the beginning of their conversation and made her fear that the other members of the community might overhear more than they would have the good sense to keep to themselves.

"God makes Himself known," Sister Lucinie said

156

firmly. "One's certainty about Him is not clear, I mean to say that it is not easy to express. He compels a lifting up of the entire being, a straining toward Him, almost a halting of the principal physiological functions. Your whole body waits for what cannot be attained, while realizing that the next contact can but destroy it, that the soul can know only at the price of its earthly life, of its independence. When God draws near, it is impossible not to know that He has come. You understand by something other than by the thoughts of human logic. It wells up in you, from all your fibers, rushing forth like lava from a volcano."

She paused. Her words transformed the room into a chapel. Mother Cécile mentally recited a Hail Mary.

"The greatness, the immensity, the threat to your existence," continued Sister Lucinie in a still lower tone, "carry you away, hold you prisoner, call to you. Your terror becomes transformed into a joyous desire as the weight of His presence disappears. You are worn out and terrified, yet attentive to the One who is leaving you. You, in turn, call out to Him, and your voice, which fears to get an answer, is lost in desperation in the void."

"But God, what do you know about God?"

She knew more than she had expressed, yet was lapsing into silence. Mother Cécile was absolutely determined to compel her to speak.

"I know nothing of God," Sister Lucinie said quietly.

The room resumed its shape before her eyes. The ochre walls, the little crucifix, and the table of white wood sprang up and took form in the half-darkness caused by the closed shutters. The nun turned her head to look at the Pope's picture and everything was again normal; but this normality, this tiny woman leaning forward to catch her words, this warm and light-lined half-darkness were for her an empty night. "I love You," she prayed in the depth of her soul; "please come to see me again." She made a welcoming gesture, then her hands fell loosely by her sides. She joined them on her knees, bending her head and her entire body in a humble and tired motion.

"There is no more to say," she added. "I have told you everything."

Now her breathing was more relaxed, as if alone. Mother Cécile continued her questioning.

"Do you prepare for these apparitions by some special self-discipline, or do they come to you completely unanticipated?"

"The states of expectation and of receptivity occur of their own accord, once you are aware that God is approaching. He does not show Himself when you wish, but at the hour He chooses. He appears in a flash."

"Wait a moment," the Superior said, seeking clarification. "You say you are conscious that He is coming, that you wait for Him, then that He appears in a flash. Is that not a contradiction?"

"Perhaps," Sister Lucinie admitted.

She wanted only one thing, to renew the moment that had just passed, to return to Him, to rejoin God, and every word was taking her farther away, scattering her fragile memories of the Divine. What difference did it make whether the Superior believed or disagreed? Was it not better to abandon the entire effort, to adopt once more the appearance of indifference she had shown earlier? Did the rule require truth or obedience? Sister

158

Lucinie had no desire to rebel. She sought no distinction. On the contrary, she wanted to be lost in the mass. And yet, if she failed to explain, was she not betraying God?

"No," she continued. Her voice had recovered its natural tone, and her soul no longer fought to retain the emotions of the past minutes. "No, there is no contradiction. The warning signs occur without my looking for them, but they take place so slowly that I am able to put myself in a state of receptivity."

"How long does that last?"

Sister Lucinie looked carefully at the Superior. She could not believe that God had come and that the other had noticed nothing, had suspected nothing. A first movement of subdued anger seized her, then she recalled that she herself was seldom aware of God and that nevertheless He existed everywhere and at all times. She answered:

"I have no idea. The time of God's arrival and presence seems to me to be quite long, and the movement of the soul seems instantaneous and involuntary. But I have no real basis for measurement. To escape into the infinite means to stop counting."

"Why should that be? Does the contemplation of God absorb you so utterly?"

"No," said Sister Lucinie, forced by her own probing to realize more clearly what she had experienced, "what happens is that the infinite gives no point of reference in time. You experience the eternity of the moment in God. There are, of course, the moments before the departure and after the return that can help you to calculate, yet your reckoning is false because eternity and

159

minutes as we know them on earth have no common measure."

"Then you believe that time passes more slowly up there than down here?"

"It is not a question of up there or down here, but of God," Sister Lucinie explained patiently, "and time does not pass, for there is no way to calculate it. Unchangeable in His apparent immobility, He does not show Himself when He is absent. We are, and that's all. We do not reflect."

Mother Cécile made a gesture of helplessness. She no longer followed Sister Lucinie. She was unable to partake of her experience. This questioning was making her tired, and she was suddenly conscious of her age.

"When have you seen that most recently?"

She could not bring herself to mention God's name. The inadequate definitions that the young woman had given her, the pursuit of exactness in the analysis of an occurrence so extremely subtle, began to convince her. A vague, scarcely discernible fear was taking shape.

Sister Lucinie smiled sweetly.

"I do not see God, He makes Himself felt, He makes Himself understood. And I have just felt Him, right here in front of you, almost this very moment."

Mother Cécile studied her subordinate. She looked very much like anyone else. Even the unusual smile that stressed the sad softness of her face did not suggest any special sign of grace. Nevertheless, they both experienced, or at least Mother Cécile experienced, a feeling of uneasiness as regards Sister Lucinie that was hard to put into words, an uneasiness that seemed to the Mother Visitatrix to parallel the concern of Mother

Dominique, the admiration of Sister Perpétue, and the love of Sister Anne of the Cross. All these feelings were mingled and reflected in the attitude of the Mother General. "Don't do anything to hurt her," she had urged. "I place great hope in her. If you continue to doubt, send her to me. I'll accept responsibility for her."

Mother Cécile was already forming in her mind a picture of their eventual departure. She no longer doubted that this nun was equally incapable of deceiving herself or of lying, but nevertheless she could not see how a contact with God could occur in such silence and with such self-control.

Chapter XVIII

SISTER JEANNE, Sister Pélagie, and Sister Perpétue no longer engaged in private conversation with Sister Lucinie. They had examined her room, confiscated her black notebook, and forbidden her to visit the town. She felt in Sister Dominique's behavior a forced severity completely at variance with her character, and she had ceased to receive from Sister Anne of the Cross the little evidences of affection to which she had grown accustomed.

All of this created around her an increased silence which she would have loved were it not for the feeling of guilt it aroused. The hostility or rather the new distrust of the community tired her out. She did not believe that she deserved punishment, feeling that her isolation represented rather a hygienic precaution for the sake of the others than chastisement for her behavior. Without rebelling against Mother Cécile's decision, without abandoning any of her activities, and without disclosing her grief in complaints or looking for a way to upset her, she buried herself in a night of silence and sorrow.

She avoided the others to make it easier for them, throwing herself into manual work even though it did not suffice to fill all her moments and free her from her thoughts. When she examined herself, she ended up by feeling that she had been guilty of an error of judgment. She believed that her knowledge of God did not run in normal channels, and she was torn between her desire to be faithful to her religion and her desire to reach divine truth. She imagined that she only had to accept this presence, to die and be absorbed into it, in order to end every constraint and every limit. Yet she rejected this solution, no longer for fear of physical death, for her body had ceased to protest, or for love of life, for she no longer believed in her mission as a nurse and knew that any of the other sisters could replace her, but from a hesitant and troubled refusal that she had difficulty in understanding.

Today she was scrubbing the concrete floor of the little courtyard, making a tremendous effort to remove some stains by working on them with a coarse brush. Only her hands were busy. Her mind was free, even though she was moving around all the time, hosing and working her brush under every flowerpot, in all the corners, and around the gray sink. Everything gradually took on the fresh smell of damp earth and running water. She

163

scrubbed the big gray flagstones on which Sister Dominique set out the green-leaved plants, whatever kind they happened to bring her, making for herself a setting like that of her childhood — a tiny garden assembled on metal shelves attached to the walls, where very few flowers, occasionally some geraniums, succeeded in blooming.

The water splashed on all sides gave a festival air to this insignificant corner of the house. As she watched the leaves of a palm bend under the spray, Sister Lucinie recalled the joy of the vine in the country and realized that the great current of love existing in the material world was likewise present here. Every plant stretched itself, trembling, from the frail asparagus to the pallid fern that sprouted at the top of the pyramid. This happiness poured over onto the metal frames and onto the flagstones, which were already absorbing the water and drying. It swelled up along the walls bathed in golden sunlight, touched the colored panes in the doors, and escaped through the red expanse of the chapel's stained-glass window to reach the sky that bent down to meet it in a tender greeting.

Mother Cécile was worried. With no clue to what was passing through the nun's mind she watched from behind the window in the corridor door this too striking, too pure, and too transparent profile, which lighted up with a mysterious smile, took part in the ecstasy of the courtyard, and finally found rest. Sister Lucinie's whole behavior disturbed her, just as did that of the community. The young woman's excessive wisdom, her total submission, the extreme vigor with which she governed her appetite and all her behavior troubled the Visitatrix, just as did the silent flame and grief of the other three sisters and the vigorously expressed fury of Sister Anne of the Cross. In spite of the absolute obedience on every side, she somehow felt herself cast in the role of executioner. She was not sure that she was doing the right thing. Sister Lucinie gave no opening for criticism. She followed the convent rule perfectly, remained so quietly in the background that it was not easy to keep an eye on her, never complained. Her work as a nurse was perfect. Mother Cécile could not confirm this point from her own observation, for she kept her home and forbade all outside work, but Mother Dominique's assurance would have sufficed without the confirmation of constant calls from the sick for her help.

Nevertheless, the old nun was unwilling to end Sister Lucinie's isolation. She had reservations about this calm, this extreme abstemiousness, and this lack of facility in prayer. She found no evidence of a deep secret, and even this increased her doubts. She had expected to meet a nun completely immersed in prayer and had been pulled up short, shocked, indeed, on finding an untiring floor scrubber, an excellent ironer and cook. Even this smile just flickering on the penitent's lips, her first expression of joy since Mother Cécile's arrival, did not inspire her to bless herself or to pray. She did not go to the chapel when her work ended, but to the kitchen or terrace.

As a matter of fact, after playing a moment with a spiked cactus, Sister Lucinie arranged her tools and scraped her shoes on the doormat. A moment later Mother Cécile heard her starting the coal fire.

The young woman loved every corner of the house.

For her it was home, a place of safety and affection. She knew that this love would accompany her from convent to convent, no matter where the Mother General sent her. Today, nevertheless, it was leaving her. She did not feel her customary joy when using these tools. Neither was her reaction one of distaste nor even of tiredness, but an indifference that simply allowed her to do her work correctly. She had not lost her power over them. They were still her tools, this her community, but she belonged to them only up to a point. She was detaching her emotions, leaving with the convent simply her services and her good will. Every tie was loosening, and still this liberated love was not going toward God. It seemed to dissolve rather than accumulate in a reserve, and the nun felt a great void develop inside her. This act, the courage of this act and of this acceptance that she did not dare offer to God, made her more alone than had Mother Cécile's decision.

A part of her soul felt sorry for the soul itself, and her refusal was born of her desire to retain her individuality before God. One day she would die and her body would dissolve in the earth, never to reappear in its present form. She looked forward with indifference to this future, but she struggled to retain the individuality of her soul. She had to live in God and for God, even in the afterlife, but retaining her identity, existing in relation to earthly contacts, and knowing that she remained Sister Lucinie and would not be lost in God who was changeless in His wisdom and His existence.

But this desire expressed itself as a prayer and a request, not as a wish.

Chapter XIX

SISTER LUCINIE slowed down to keep in step with Mother Cécile. It seemed silly to her to drag the old nun along a lot of dusty roads just to show her the district welfare office, a cold and comfortless spot, and so far away. Her frail companion had trouble in keeping up with her. Each time they passed a tree, she halted, panting, in the shade. Sister Lucinie grudged the long delays, but she had given up trying to understand the mind of the Visitatrix. She tolerated her presence, accepted it, at times even forgot it. The heat forced her, however, to pay attention. It was her duty to wait and help this poor wasted body with a few encouraging words.

Mother Cécile seemed at the end of her tether. She

leaned against the trunk of a plantain, shut her black umbrella, and propped her head against Sister Lucinie. This action embarrassed both of them. It took from the older woman's dignity or at least stressed her weakness, while giving her young companion a protective air that amused her though she was careful to hide it. In addition, the attitude indicated that she wanted to talk, and Sister Lucinie thought that a public road, even a deserted one, was no place for conversation. Besides, to linger in the direct glare of the sun would complete Mother Cécile's exhaustion. Sister Lucinie was tempted to take her by the arm, scold her like a naughty child, and force her to drag herself to the relative coolness of the welfare center.

She had, however, exacted from herself a promise not to create any obstacle between the delegate of the motherhouse and herself, to act only under obedience, waiting patiently for whatever explanation of her anxiety she might finally offer. But Mother Cécile continued to keep her views to herself, and Sister Lucinie's patience was turning to indifference. Receiving neither blame nor help, but only silence and solitude on all sides, she was being driven deeper into her thoughts, approaching the point of ceasing to hope for any human intervention between God and herself.

She felt no irritation at any of Mother Cécile's questions, sometimes surprising herself at the speed with which she answered and the ease with which she avoided doctrinal points in which her ideas of God might possibly clash with the Church's teaching. The things about which the old Superior asked raised no problem for her. She was not concerned about the origin of Christ or the sacraments or the power of the Blessed Virgin. She accepted all such matters. She believed Jesus to be the Son of God. She believed in the help that the Church gives the believer, in the power of prayer, in the resurrection of the soul, and eternal life.

But she did not share with Mother Cécile her concepts regarding the identity of the earthly soul and the future soul, nor her certainty about the transformation of the flesh, nor about this universal intermingling that she dreaded with all her being. If Mother Cécile had objected that God can do anything, she could only have answered: "Yes, but He does in fact only what He chooses, and even our uncertain and ill-based knowledge, still subject to man's imagination and his desires, reveals to us already a part of this material order in motion toward uniformity, forecasting the end of the kind of life now lived by the earth and the world."

Sister Lucinie could not have convinced the old Superior by such arguments and ran the risk of hurting her and raising new doubts in her mind. For this reason she did not use them, making no claim to special knowledge.

Her attitude from the time of the quarrel in January up to her confession to Sister Anne of the Cross had resulted from a moral weakness the results of which she had been unable to compensate for. On entering the convent, she had undertaken to follow a rule that obliged her to answer a superior's questions candidly. She would continue to do so, but under the smooth-stemmed plantain she decided not to go beyond the obligations of obedience and no longer to reveal what she could hide without violating it.

169

But time was passing and the little Superior continued to mop her face. Sister Lucinie thought of the sick girl waiting for her and of the humble and plain face of the older sister who had come for her.

"Daughter," the Superior asked, "why was this woman so anxious that you should come?"

The anxiety and suspicion implied by the question crept painfully over the nun.

"I have no idea," she said in a low voice, thinking of herself as a nameless sister among the others with no special quality to distinguish her. "The reason may be that I helped at the center to distribute soup to the poor during the winter. She is one of a family of railroad workers and her mother is the caretaker at the center. I understand she is a member of a Third Order and did not become a nun because of poor health. It is not she but her young sister who is ill."

She stopped talking as they continued their journey. Their steps raised little puffs of red-brown dust that splashed back on their shoes.

"It must be slippery here when it rains," Mother Cécile remarked.

A mixed feeling of distrust and calm took hold of the old woman. The peace flowed from this serious companion, the doubts from her own heart. It would have been easy to believe, as the others did, that Sister Lucinie was a saint, and thus be carried along a dangerous road. It would likewise have been easy to reject her out of hand, to recall the fainting spell the day she arrived, ' and the nun's own doubts as reported by Sister Anne of the Cross. Such facts gave weight to the theory that

170

undue sensitivity and nervousness underlay a phenomenon strictly of physiological origin. Or it would also be easy to take Sister Lucinie back to the motherhouse and let the Mother General in her wisdom decide. None of these three possible solutions satisfied her. She continued to watch, while fearing that by prolonging the situation she might either contract the same contagion as others and believe against all evidence, or offend God by letting her doubts continue longer than they should. The memory of the torments inflicted on St. Teresa and St. John of the Cross did nothing to ease her scruples, and Sister Lucinie's personality was too attractive for the old woman not to come occasionally under its spell, as had happened just now, when she was distracted from her investigation by the hardship of the journey in the broiling sun.

Sister Lucinie nodded in agreement, then returned to the subject of the previous conversation.

"She is a miserable, weak-willed old maid who has sunk to the lowest depths of religion, as a person might sink to the bottom of a well of ignorance. What I mean," she explained in answer to a protesting gesture from Mother Cécile, "is that her faith is smothered in a thousand superstitions and in a fatalism that prevents her from living in society. She does practically nothing. She plays the harmonium in the chapel, extinguishes the candles, knits her scarves, and that's all."

"But," Mother Cécile protested gently, "is that not the kind of life that God loves?"

"No," Sister Lucinie said with conviction. Much as she hated it, the same anger always seized her when she came in contact with this kind of Christian security.

171

Now, however, she immediately regained her self-control. "She refuses too many of the obligations that properly go with her life. Without her sister's help, she would not be able to provide for her family's needs or her own. God placed us on earth to forget ourselves in Him and in others."

"What do you think of the contemplative orders?" Mother Cécile asked.

The neutral tone exposed a snare, and bitterness rose again inside Sister Lucinie. Would she always be under suspicion, not knowing if in fact she constituted a danger, not knowing either if she was deceived in her relations with the other world? She sighed. Such things could be overcome only in the silence of her soul and made clear in intimate contact with the divine. Why should she defend herself or try to convince? She sought no earthly glory. Her joy and her light came from elsewhere, and nothing could take them from her, since she drank at the source of happiness and had only to let herself swim with the current. What difference did threats or solitary confinement make to her?

"Your question raises a different subject. This woman does not belong to a contemplative order. I believe, of course, that contemplative orders are necessary, because I believe in the power of prayer. I attribute to them a strength created by the number of those praying together. As I see it, one finds in churches and convents an aura or spiritual force not present elsewhere, which enables mankind to find points of contact with God more easily. But this woman had not received from Providence the right to participate in that force. God has kept her in her own home, and accordingly she should

172

do what she is supposed to do. To work, to overcome sloth, and to deny oneself pleasure are also paths to sanctity."

"And her sister is not like her?"

The threat was retreating. Since Mother Cécile had come, the nun had known these alternating moments of anxiety and confidence, and ordinarily she returned quite quickly to a state of peace. Today, nevertheless, she retained a sense of anticipation in the presence of the Superior, partly from choice and partly because she found it harder to reach her former interior calm.

"No," she explained. "I only saw her once, but I recall her extreme youth. There must be a considerable number of years between them, perhaps as many as fifteen. I know that she did all the work in the house. But we are almost there, and I think they are watching out for us."

Their path took them by a yellow wall without a window, with an entrance door slightly ajar at one end. A child about twelve years old shouted abruptly to them: "My aunt is dead." Sister Lucinie pushed the little girl gently in front of her toward the courtyard. Mother Cécile walked on under the olive trees, oppressed by the wailing and weeping that reached her from the house. A great sorrow welled up inside her and overwhelmed her because she had prevented Sister Lucinie from coming earlier. She realized that she had been subconsciously hoping for the possibility of some sort of miracle for which it was now too late, and she felt herself becoming as ready in her misery to clutch at any blind faith as were little Sister Perpétue and Sister Anne of the Cross.

The little girl came with them to show the way. She held in her fingers, without a trace of shyness, the end of Sister Lucinie's beads, and she went ahead proudly to introduce them into her domain. "The pastor is here already," she announced. They were all standing around the dead girl, laid out in the burial habit, the brother, the dumbfounded father, the weeping mother, the priest, and the old maid in black with her yellowish face.

And God remained silent, showing no tenderness or purpose. The nun had no sign from Him since the day after the storm. She knew He was present within her, but He remained aloof, watching to see how she would act, just as Mother Cécile watched.

Today the question for her no longer was whether to accept the weight and the knowledge of God, but through the night, which concealed the work, to accept or reject God's action in the complex system of earthly existence, to discover the way of His wisdom, to decide if what was required of her was an absolute passive obedience and an unreflecting submission purified of all regret, or freedom, this fragmentary freedom of choice that spiritually transforms an action for good or evil at the pleasure of man rather than that of God, a freedom that at this moment might seem to operate against what apparently was the divine design.

The helpless people stood at the other side of the bed, like members of a parade headed by the gossipy priest who remained unmoved by the colossal presence. They desperately needed this dead girl, and Sister Lucinie's future was at stake in the matter.

Nevertheless, affected by the deep silence of this pale woman with the wide-brimmed cornette, they fell silent one by one, surprised by her meditative appearance. She waited for something without knowing what, perhaps a revealing or approving sign. God was silent. She thought that in the darkness of her distress she could go against the order of self-effacement, that her pity and her personality could make a stand against a system established by law, and that if she did so she might suffer the penalty of driving God away from her. He made a movement as though to disappear. "No," she groaned within herself, "I love you."

For the last time she measured the intensity of her affection, but God remained. He would stay with her until she had made her choice, and she hesitated, wounded, before this miserable family. Mother Cécile came toward her, but Sister Lucinie stopped her with a gesture, and they stood facing each other with the bed between them. The room was charged with tension, ready to burst under the tremendous pressure. The young woman alone recognized this power while the others doubled under its weight and knew that none but she could help. Once more she turned toward the dead girl and hesitated. She felt this mass encompass and crush her heart and her brow. Her hand raised itself painfully. Now she could act and pay for her act.

She saw nothing more, her hand remaining stretched over the young woman, bringing back her breath, concentrated on God who was going away, fading in a tender caress like a fresh breeze on her face. Then, slowly, the excited voice of the priest and the grateful words of the relatives and of Mother Cécile reached her.

Chapter XX

THE TRAIN had rolled for hours across the dreary desert of barren earth, its gray face gashed by the sun, unrelieved by a farmhouse or even a tent. Occasionally it stopped at a parched station, and Sister Lucinie would ask herself how and why a town should exist there, the white houses gathered about their water source. Then the couplings would creak and the coaches would resume their monotonous movement.

The two nuns were jammed together in a corner of the compartment. Mother Cécile, sitting between Sister Lucinie and the other passengers, was half-covered by the woolen garment in which the man sitting next to her was swathed. At times his sleeping head fell on her shoulder and she did not dare stir, although nauseated by the sight of five or six fleas that wandered at random in the folds of his turban and cloak. At such times Sister Lucinie would poke the sleeping man and push away his indiscreet garments without daring to suggest again that they should exchange places, since the Superior had steadfastly refused to do so since morning. She watched the landscape slide past, always looking for the blue-gray snow-capped mountains whose slender peaks loomed against the horizon. The evening faded slowly and now all that remained was a long line of gold on the black earth. When the band of light turned to a soft violet, then to a pastel green, and faded away, the last words also faded into silence on the train.

Sister Lucinie forced Mother Cécile to take the seat by the door, and while the old woman slept, her hands clasped around her black bag, she listened to a group of young Jews crouching or stretched on the corridor floor who from time to time wakened up to chat and eat pomegranates. She did not understand their language, and their faces, scarcely visible in the dim glow of the night lights, did not arouse her curiosity. They were alive and she could hear them, and that sufficed to hold her attention. She tried in vain to arouse some interest in her trip. But it produced neither pleasure nor regret. The memory of the little house, of Sister Jeanne's shining staircase and of the cell where her agony had been born, evaporated without a pang.

The events of the past three weeks, the court of inquiry established by the Bishop, the interrogations, all of this was dropping behind, carrying with it every sense of bitterness and shame. Only an emptiness free of pain survived from the nightmare. But this calm did not hide the memory of the miracle. They had succeeded in making her say that the young girl must have been in a state of lethargy, and sometimes even in making her believe it. Nevertheless, in this sultry October night, loud with the rhythmic complaints of the tie rods and the wheels, she reaffirmed this death and this resurrection. Proof of the reality of the miracle remained secondary for her. God had not tried a group appeal, He simply sought to draw the nun toward Himself, perhaps to subject her to some trials and give her a new kind of understanding.

He had provided a double contact with the death she dreaded, an opportunity to understand it by making her interfere with its action. But Sister Lucinie was not concerned with order or logic. Pity alone had clashed with death, even after she had accepted Madame Senlis's destiny. What had happened in that case was that emotional disturbance had taken charge and was leading to a destruction of the conscience as complete as that of the body. Madeleine's reason for wanting to die was to save her soul. She had gone without offering resistance. This last expression clarified things for Sister Lucinie. The compassion that drove her and through which she had gone against God's apparent design sought, on the contrary, a way of obedience in accord with divine wisdom, not the satisfaction of life but a way for the soul to reach a higher degree of sanctity.

Perhaps she had done the right thing, but she feared that this tardy analysis did not justify her action. She wept in the darkness of the coach because her intelligence and her love did not maintain the same rhythm.

Sister Lucinie no longer saw anything outside except a long line of lights projected on the rocky banks where

178

the earth rose high on each side of the tracks. Slowly she returned to her previous thoughts.

Her fear of death produced moments of doubt and moments of irritation. At times she succeeded in drowning it out. But it still existed. She believed in God and looked forward to uniting herself with Him. No longer did she want to preserve her body, yet she feared to lose her identity in death, or at least that was how she had seen it up to a moment ago. Actually, as she had just suddenly come to realize, she did not want to retain the special personality of Sister Lucinie but, even anonymously and absorbed in the divine mass, a separate soul that would retain the same Christian virtues she had in life sought to acquire. Her humanity remained alive within her and rose up against a different God.

Yet she loved God. She loved Him from childhood with so complete an affection that no other love had held her with the same force or so blindly, so that all subsequent knowledge and moral teaching were merely superimposed artificially without modifying her attitude, without deepening or clarifying it.

She had doubted God's existence and meaning without ever ceasing to love Him, even if her love had not always been clearly visible. It had hidden itself at times so deeply as to plunge her into doubt, then had swelled up again in great waves in the tumult of a violent emotion or in the calm of her thought, as it was doing tonight in the creaking train that carried her through this unknown and somber countryside.

The sweaty sleep of the travelers or the monotonous rhythm of the wheels could not prevent a flowering of sweetness and an uplifting of the soul in joy, a sense of

179

expectation of a strange tenderness, or the sound of an anticipated voice that did not answer her call. She watched in the night and slowly approached a darkened station, covered with bougainvillaea, where her trip ended.

Chapter XXI

SISTER LUCINIE stayed a little behind the others, listening to the gentle splash of water in the fountain. She barely distinguished the faces turned toward Mother Cécile, and took little interest in the questions asked. Names were mentioned and items of news that she already knew were exchanged about the other far-off house where life continued without her. In her mind's eye she could see Sister Anne of the Cross on her knees in the chapel, her old heart broken with sorrow, her wrinkled hand waiting for the pressure of Sister Lucinie's fingers it had so seldom received. She heard Sister Pélagie whisper: "I feel strong when you touch me," and little Sister Perpétue: "It's good to be near you." And Sister Jeanne, Sister Jeanne who must have hidden her notebook of poems the first time they had gone through her room, and who had given it back to her quietly just as she was leaving.

She could no longer join them in prayer. She had ceased to be a member of that group, and the eight women who surrounded her here did not present a like family unity. Mother Cécile, too, was becoming more remote, letting her slide away toward complete abandonment, and Sister Lucinie accepted this indifference and solitude in which she could live from now on without enduring the weight of beings loved too greatly. Her only desire was to find God again. He had not shown Himself since the miracle at the welfare center; and she was filled with a passionate longing when she recalled the ecstasy. Love built up within her, offering itself as a gift, rejecting the sadness of the past, and finally accepting God in His truth and His might. But it had not succeeded in destroying her fear. It would perhaps be easier, she thought, as she sat in the center of the courtyard tiled to half the height of its walls, to subdue it by an act of the will than to eliminate it by reasoning. She did not yet feel herself ready, but she did want to reach God.

A cat rubbed against her, passed from her skirt to that of another nun, and jumped on her knees. Sister Paule made him welcome, running her hand along the flowing line of his spine. Mother Cécile frowned but said nothing. Sister Lucinie recognized that she did not change. Her technique was always the same, first a probe, then a thrust. Mother Cécile could no longer hurt Sister Lucinie, but she had the traits of a cruel examiner. Sister Pélagie, too, would remember her experience.

Who would be the object of her attack here? Sister

Paule without a doubt, and Sister Agnes, too, whose shoes in spite of the dispensation from the strict rule were not in keeping with the habit. But would she also try to sound the soul of the fourth nun seated near the fountain, a hard-faced woman who repelled Sister Lucinie? The young nun asked herself if she could, supernaturally, penetrate the consciences of the nuns gathered in the courtyard. In that case, the miracle would unfold inside her, without witnesses. Whether she succeeded or failed, she would arouse no anger, but she would make use for no good purpose of a power that did not belong to her. God bestowed it on her but she much preferred to give than to receive. This was the only way she knew how to love, forgetting herself and giving herself completely. This, she hoped, would enable her to conquer her fear and slowly and naturally to achieve a maturity that would purify her in the act of transforming her. It was easy to inflict pain on oneself, and then, when it had become impossible to remove or diminish it, to bear it bravely, but it was harder to change a forced consent into a precious joy.

Would her stay in this unknown town enable her to reach peace? She recognized a threat in this overcrowded collection of houses, these narrow little streets, these endless native markets, these reed-covered passages where treasures were piled up in unbelievable abundance and confusion, this endless jostling of porters, merchants, students, and artisans, this medley of natives and Europeans. Her uneasiness arose not from the differences between these last two groups but from their similarities, from the sway of the earth over both, the indelible mark of the country.

She felt them rise up abruptly in solidly packed crowds

183

in her imagination, and the sight blotted out her eight companions, the fountain, and the tiled walls, moving in time to the rhythm of a swing tune being played somewhere in the neighborhood. The vision mocked her, dividing itself into innumerable arms stretched out in gestures of supplication, prayer, and threat. Now the very ground shook. The earth, the people, and the trees and flowers all converged on Sister Lucinie in a confused and crazy dance, like a series of processions approaching from every direction. They melted away in the distance, always replaced by others. They stamped the ground, rising and falling in great waves, coming down toward her from mountaintops, drawing her up to terrifying heights. And night enveloped this monstrous movement, provoking noisy confusion, changing and tightening the giant tentacles in an interminable howling.

Then, quite suddenly, the gentle silence, the murmur of the water and the voices, and the solitude in the midst of the community blotted out the noise. Sister Paule still played with her cat. The Superior of the community sitting upright, spoke in her dry way while nobody listened, and Mother Cécile sank down in her chair and raised apprehensive eyes toward Sister Lucinie.

Chapter XXII

AFTER a few days of rest Sister Lucinie felt the need to resume work. She found it good once more to use up her energies, to devote all her strength to fighting sickness, to revive joy in someone, and to forget a little of the excessively strong call, the love that filled her yet escaped her, the never-satisfied anticipation. But for some months she had adopted an attitude of silence which by cloistering her soul made her agitated and timid. She felt that her former self-assurance had fled, and she now doubted her ability as a nurse, fearing that she could not adapt herself to new customs.

Sister Monique brought her through the labyrinth of little streets to the broad highways of the new town. Sister Lucinie was amazed at the open spaces, the broad sidewalks, the spacious modern homes surrounded by concrete balconies, and the luxurious doorways. The city gave an impression of wealth that had not been visible in the little town far away and already almost forgotten. The nun tried to recall the straight streets cut at right angles, and the stores all in a row.

Sister Monique turned into an avenue that stretched away under trees between two rows of villas hidden by terraced gardens. She stopped before a wooden side gate and Sister Lucinie read the brass plate.

"Here we are," Sister Monique remarked. "I shall come back for you in the afternoon. In Mademoiselle Lambert you have a very bad-tempered patient, a young woman who once had infantile paralysis. You will see how it has affected her. Today her mother diagnosed influenza. She finds a new sickness for her every time the nurse changes. We are often called in as substitutes, and, as you will see, it's not funny."

They followed a path that wound between pine trees and clusters of flowers. The villa gave the same impression as the city — a display of luxury and a waste of space. Inside, the tapestries, the ornaments of beaten bronze, the paintings, and the carved furniture fulfilled the promise of the outside. Uniformed servants in carefully wound turbans moved about phlegmatically in deep silence.

The nuns went upstairs to the patient's bedroom, and Sister Lucinie was amazed to find another manservant making the bed. The girl, seated in an invalid chair, followed every slightest movement. She listened to Sister Monique and dismissed her with a cold gesture. Sister Lucinie remained standing, listening to a running criticism of the servant. He, however, took no notice, going ahead with his work in his own way, making no effort to hurry. The nun was upset by the invalid's unpleasant way of giving orders, as well as by watching this work that she had never before seen done by a man and the indifference, verging on insolence, of the native. The entire performance revolted her.

The invalid never looked at the nun. She had not even done her the courtesy of greeting her. It was obvious that she sought to establish her uselessness. A sudden anger took possession of Sister Lucinie and she dismissed the valet. "It's my practice to do the cleaning myself," she said. "I don't allow any servants around me."

She prepared the bath, rolled back the carpets, and swept the floor with a speed that amazed the sick girl, who stopped complaining to watch the worker, amazed at the effort she expended and at the silent determination, stronger than her own desire to reduce her companion to a condition of superfluity. When everything was done, Sister Lucinie sat down near Mademoiselle Lambert and took some work out of her bag. She was embroidering an altar cloth like the one she had made in the other convent, lovingly filling each grain of the stylized ears of wheat.

The vigorous efforts she had just expended filled her with a deep satisfaction she had not felt for a long time. She found herself in these earthly and human activities. She was a normal woman, and she looked squarely at last at the fear of what was strange and abnormal that had pursued her for months. But she recognized that she was still the same nun she had always been. She was making peace with herself, both with her mind and with the possibilities of her flesh, and this fact also brought an increase of love and joy.

It was as if God and her soul, coming by different roads, had looked for Sister Lucinie and had found themselves in her. The song of her members and her heart followed the same ascent as had that of the vine, and her body revealed itself as similar to the vine stock and the earth. Her happiness came from her knowledge of God. Long ago He had received the soul of the young woman and illuminated it in each of her fibers which were at the same time strangers to each other and intimately united. Only the soul understood. She held herself at the frontier of this communion with envy, astonishment, and happiness. Since half of her person partook of the enchantment, she also followed. She no longer knew what fixed her boundaries, and she sought to rediscover this God who had reached her before she was aware of it.

She felt ready to sing in spite of the uneasiness she felt because of the absence of the patient's parents. She had often found hostility to or impatience with the sick, never this total indifference. As there was no woman servant in the house, the man in the room on her arrival must have got the girl out of bed in the morning. Sister Lucinie shuddered as she thought of the frail and deformed body in the hard arms of the native. She did not understand how anyone could surrender like this to the care of valets or servants, forgetting all shame, and treating the hired help as of so little consequence as to lose all sense of a human relationship between master and servant.

She felt sorry for the girl abandoned amid such luxury,

then remembered that a nurse usually tended her and that only the bitterness of her own character drove the nurses away. She recalled the tone of voice she had heard earlier, and when she looked at the sick girl, she recognized the same discontented and bitter look. Then her pity melted into grief, and she revolted against the spirit of pride and hatred that she felt flowing from the girl. The patient's scorn flooded over her like a viscous ectoplasm and she refused interiorly to accept it. Christian humility could play no part in this, for it would very easily deteriorate into laziness, and Sister Lucinie did not believe that she herself was personally committed. The concrete fact was that the soul of the commandant's daughter was crawling around in misery, and it was important to free it. The nun did not know how to do this, and her desire to bring peace to her companion did not express itself with sufficient force to keep her constantly on the watch. On the contrary, she felt a need to postpone action, to escape in her mind from these unduly rich surroundings, and to return to the sources of love.

All she had to do was to pronounce the divine Name and form in her mind an image of one of His powers in order to regain a somewhat apprehensive joy, a tender impulse mixed with anguish, the ecstasy-filled doubt of the one in love in the presence of her silent lover, a new Psyche anxious to know God. But she did not again dare to go outside the realm of feeling, to project her thoughts into the unknown. Now it was enough to love.

Sister Lucinie looked at the invalid. Marie-Reine Lambert was crying from anger because of her weakness. The nun realized the girl's humiliation and her cruel desire to hurt. She laid a gentle hand on her.

"Would you like me to sing something for you?" she asked.

She waited for the patient's bitterness to subside under the touch of her hand, then she began to sing the Pentecost cantata. Her original intention disappeared. She forgot the house and its sleeping owners and let her emotions expand within her, Bach's music stirring them to the very depths of her being. It was not God who threatened her today. Rather her own extremely fierce love carried her to the edge of death, and she could not break off this song which she found herself uncontrollably urged to continue to the very last words. When she finished, her whole body was trembling with an internal movement not visible in her motionless face and hands or in her absolutely rigid arms.

She felt the dark, watching eyes of the girl, and she smiled at her. Nevertheless, her cheeks and forehead retained the reflection of her dangerous inspiration, and Mademoiselle Lambert followed attentively the last reflections of this state. She did not know just how far Sister Lucinie would venture, not understanding the precise quality of her emotion, but she sensed something more powerful than the song and more mystic than the words, namely, a superhuman appeal, and she believed that God had answered because her desolate soul felt the presence of an unaccustomed melancholy.

All her anger forgotten, she was drawn to Sister Lucinie as to a haven of consolation, and with halting words she unburdened the bitterness bred by her illness, the longing to be like the others, and the need her heart felt for love.

Sister Lucinie kept her grip on the girl's hand while

190

the burning grief built up inside her, and once again the temptation to perform a miracle seized her. She could raise this living creature from the corruption in which she was sunk and give her a chance still to be saved, but she did not want to act against God. Unable to understand His too unyielding wisdom, all she wanted was to submit. The persecutions she had suffered since her intervention at the community center did not enter into her decision. All of that remained on the human level, faded into the background, and ceased to appear real. There remained only this sick girl whose limbs were paralyzed, and her own will to obey.

The nun's silence, nevertheless, surprised Mademoiselle Lambert. She felt tired from her outpourings, the emotion of the song, and the fear of causing displeasure. Her nurse fascinated her, and she gave herself over completely, relinquishing her independence because the young nun's pity permitted her to feel understood and loved. God formed for her a certainty, but she seldom thought about Him. She kept Him in the background of her spiritual life, with none of that deep transport that Sister Lucinie's song had just awakened, for it was this music, not merely Bach's work but also what the singer's voice added to it, that had caused her awakening.

"God could cure me if He wanted to."

The nurse did not answer. An autumn wind was spreading clouds across the sky from the west. Mechanically she closed the window and placed a wrap over the withered legs. In what kind of dances would these gaunt limbs tire themselves out if they were cured? To what distant and trivial life would they bring the sick girl? What unlikely moral resurrection would they prevent?

Mademoiselle Lambert was self-sufficient because of her belief in her own superiority. If the test of illness had failed to develop forbearance, what could one hope from a normal life in which her wealth and education would sustain her pride and cruelty? Yet, on the other hand, if the momentary manifestation of Sister Lucinie's religious emotion had upset her withered spirit, the living mark of God traced on her flesh could transform the young girl for better. Everything in her pointed toward a miracle, and the strength of her prayer entered into the nun.

All that remained of the sick girl was a joyless skeleton, and to this physical semi-destruction was joined an abysmal bitterness. Sister Lucinie felt the same distress, the revolts, envy, and ill-nature grow within herself, and this terrifying whirlpool boiled up inside her, destroying her and spreading her to the extreme ends of the earth. Then again it swept her to the very border of the abode of evil, across the infinity of the world. This headlong journey and this return of the sorrow on herself established the need for boundaries. But she felt a movement and a call to go forward and to suffer that remained a submission in spite of the verbal revolt it inspired.

The voice of the patient reached the nun as she experienced these painful and hidden forces. "Sister, can He cure me?" Her answer was an involuntary prayer: "Dear Lord, cure her."

The girl's words had touched her. Ordinarily she said: "God." But today she used a term of new tenderness, "Dear Lord." She remembered the jocose and scarcely respectful words used by old Sister Anne of the Cross, Our Spouse, His harem. Was He indeed the Spouse? No, rather the lover above everything, the lover beyond anything we might be able to do, the lover in spite of our indifference, the disrupting lover whose light-filled spirituality could not be reached by any material contact.

"Could He?"

The sorrowing prayer still reached her in her flight and surprised her at the center of her love in a way in which it had failed to affect her a moment earlier in the depths of her misery. She recognized a noise that had to be stilled, a sacrilegious sorrow which, in order not to disturb the wondrous moment and to prolong the ecstasy, God appeased through the voice of His loved one. "I shall cure you."

Slowly the serene harmony died down. Terrified, Sister Lucinie found herself again in the luxurious bedroom.

"God will cure you," she corrected herself.

But what importance has man's fear? God spoke through her, God animated her.

"Get up," she ordered.

Chapter XXIII

THE NEWS of the miracle spread quickly through
the town and reached the Protestant pastor late in the
afternoon in his little flower-adorned house beside the
church built where two streets intersected, at the bottom
of a triangular garden. Pastor Vandel loved his tiny
estate and passed the most enjoyable hours of his life in
the sacristy where he kept his books.

It had been his ambition, when he came to North
Africa, to bring the gospel to the natives and thus open
a glorious path for his faith. Actually, he had not been
able to carry out this purpose and had allowed himself
to slide gradually into the mediocre setting of a Euro-
pean church whose members had no taste for the great
sacrifices of which he had dreamed.

194

This afternoon he listened with a mounting disbelief to one of his wife's friends.

"I have not seen her," she was saying. "The ecclesiastical authorities have forbidden the Lamberts to see anybody except the Lacauds, who are their relatives, and of course the higher officials whom they can't stop. Mademoiselle Lacaud told me the story. She saw Marie-Reine walking and she herself told her all about her cure."

Notwithstanding her obvious emotion, this woman he knew was nothing but a shameless gossip who ran around the town with every extravagant rumor, repeating the most unpleasant reports with childish and cruel pleasure. His wife and he welcomed her to their home only because they could not keep her out. Today they listened to her politely, thinking of their evening meal, which was going to be late, and occasionally exchanging a stealthy glance that expressed their amused contempt for these Catholic mirages.

"The nun just recently came here," the visitor went on. "I believe her name is Sister Lucy or Lucille. The detail was unimportant, so I didn't bother to ask her to repeat the name."

She noticed that her hosts looked at each other, and that now they were deeply interested.

"Are you sure of the name of the Order?" the pastor asked.

"Quite sure. It is the only one in town that sends out its members to nurse the sick in their own homes. Their convent is in the old town right in the sector of the native markets."

The detail burned into the pastor's soul. He had failed

in his wish to live among the natives, and instead he had to satisfy himself with this attractive house where everything was too bright, too new, and too easy.

"Do you happen to know her?" the visitor asked in turn.

"We are interested in all the details," Madame Vandel replied. "This story is already the talk of the town."

"Did you think what I did?" she asked her husband as soon as they were alone. "The name of the order is a coincidence, and the similarity in the nun's name is also striking."

"Yes," the pastor answered thoughtfully, "but her name in religion is Sister Lucinie, and her mother in her last letter said nothing about a transfer to a new convent."

"Do you think that miracles can happen?"

They left the question unanswered, recalling the invalid chair in which the sick girl went about town. A dull doubt assailed their certitude. There were two branches of the Vandel family, one of them Catholic and the other Protestant. From time to time there were marriages between the two branches, and Sister Lucinie was the pastor's cousin. This relationship gave her a significance that without their knowing disturbed the couple's judgment.

"I could find out a little more about it tomorrow, if you think well," Madame Vandel suggested.

"Yes," the pastor agreed. "Find out if the extraordinary happening actually took place and if the one involved was a Sister Lucy or was our cousin. If the latter proved to be the case, perhaps I should go to the parish priest to find out more about it."

Madame Vandel began to experience a suffocating joy.

"Why would you not go directly to see Sister Lucinie?"

"As a matter of protocol. We are Protestants. They might fear our influence. Later on they will undoubtedly allow you to go to see her."

A servant entered the room.

"We'll go," the mistress of the house burst out. Then she added: "John, I do hope that this is true."

The pastor spread sugar on his cheese without noticing what he was doing. He had no taste for food, a quality that pained his wife greatly, for he thus denied her talents as a cook, just as he ignored her attractiveness as a woman, her hard work, and spotless home, as befitted a Lorraine housewife, and her need to express herself in words and gestures. Since they were married, she had lost her taste for laughing and moving about, her frivolous and pleasant chattering like a bird's song, and her fondness for prettying herself up and decorating the house. But she could not shake off her pride in her cooking, and the neglect, blindness, and indifference of her husband renewed each day a grief that he never noticed, having no eye for the ordinary affairs of life.

He lived with a sense of duty, which Madame Vandel thought it would be much better to limit to the obligations imposed by the Ten Commandments. Her husband, however, felt the need to go vastly farther, although in practice external difficulties hindered his attainment of his goal. As for her, she had trouble in living up to far less demanding ideals. Though she sincerely desired to do her duty, her will was not strong enough to prevent an occasional lapse. Tiny failures often marred the perfection of the edifice, and she had no desire to be given more important tasks to perform.

Today, however, her troubles vanished before Sister Lucinie's miracle. The pastor, abandoning his usual silence, repeated enthusiastically the slightest details of his visit to the Lambert home, the arrival of the bishop, and of the Mother General of the order; the comments of the doctors and their affirmative response regarding the unforeseeable and sudden cure, as well as their anxiety to follow further development of this miraculous happening; Marie-Reine's joy and that of her parents; the attitude of the three Mothers Superior, and the ill-disguised annoyance of the bishop with the conduct of the parish priest who was half out of his mind with faith and happiness.

"I can't understand why he should blame him," Madame Vandel said thoughtfully. "In the presence of God's work, how is it possible to control one's enthusiasm? Imagine Moses before the burning bush or Elias before the blazing pyre. Do you think they kept silent?"

"No," the pastor agreed, "but the cases are different. The bishop must think of the effect on our cousin, and his prudence is proper. Such suspicion can upset us because it reflects on a relative whom we love, but he does not know her, and I agree that it is not right to jump too quickly to conclusions. Everything that belongs in the realm of science must be protected and kept separate from the divine intervention."

"Everything that belongs to science," the mistress of the house repeated unbelievingly. "But, whether it can be explained or not, everything belongs to God."

She felt all tightened up, her eyes downcast and fixed on the table top, her hands on her knees playing with a corner of the napkin. Pastor Vandel always insisted on his exclusive right to discuss God, and his wife's unanticipated intrusion startled him, but he did not think it necessary to explain the difference that arose in this occurrence between the work of God and that of man.

"Agnes's religious indifference during all her youthful years surprised them," he said. "Besides, she seems greatly changed. Her superiors knew her as a very gay and even exuberant person. Can you imagine that?"

"Agnes Vandel," the pastor's wife said in a loud voice. "It is absolutely impossible for me to think of this name as still belonging to her. For me she has definitely become Sister Lucinie. But I don't understand why you should be surprised at her gaiety. You only saw her during your visits to her parents' home, and they were extremely severe people. Don't forget that I could never laugh, either, in the presence of your uncle or your father. She was another person in the boarding school, and in spite of the difference in our ages I remember quite clearly that she took part in all the games. Besides, the religious indifference you mention was as superficial as her gravity of manner. She belonged to an almost atheistic family, and you can understand why she would never stress her views. But she went to Mass without fail every Sunday, even when she had to get up very early to do so and the school imposed no obligation. All her upbringing was of a kind to encourage her to hide her emotions, and I believe that one could live a long time with her, even at the college to which she let them

199

send her, without really knowing anything about her inner life."

"No doubt you're right."

The pastor agreed almost reluctantly. He recalled a sensible child, a very pretty little girl who spoke little and kept to herself while she pursued her university studies. He remembered the day they had said good-by. Nobody yet knew about her wish to become a nun. She congratulated him and added: "You are very lucky to be able to consecrate yourself to God." She had spoken without emotion of this opportunity that had subsequently been realized, in her rather high voice that cut through the whispers of the people standing near them, and indeed nothing in her tone indicated that what she said was more than an expression of politeness. Nevertheless, five months later she herself began her novitiate.

Pastor Vandel stood up, asking himself if he would recognize her on sight.

"Why don't you come, too," he suggested. "You seem to know her better than I do, and perhaps you would be more helpful."

"No," his wife answered bitterly. "I can't give them any help. I hate their excessive wisdom, their determination to cut her power, her holiness, and her glory down to the level of their needs. I shall go to see her if she wants me to, but only for her, and because God lives in her. Don't look at me like that. Among all these blind people, you are one of the blindest."

Chapter XXIV

SISTER LUCINIE looked at each of them in turn, studying their eyes, searching for the threat hidden in them. She did not linger on the faces of the three Mothers Superior, for she could read inside them. Their reserve hid a deep faith, and in spite of all the world's condemnations, their love would still be hers. But she feared the Bishop, and even more this young priest with the round face who accompanied him. Her cousin's presence was totally unexpected and surprised her. She no longer found in him the faith that had previously inspired him and raised him above himself. The austerity of his face was no longer that of a mystic. All it now showed was sorrow around the mouth and eyelids heavy with fatigue. The climate and weariness had conquered him.

He was watching, waiting for the same thing that she was waiting for, the tangible coming of God. All were hoping for this presence, but they expected it to flash forth from the nun as a result of the interrogation she had been enduring patiently for half an hour in the lime-washed room where, as in the other convent from which she had come, a black crucifix and a portrait of the Pope adorned the walls. Notwithstanding the similarity, Sister Lucinie failed to find here the gentleness of the other house, and after having detached herself emotionally from it to the point of almost completely forgetting it, she was again thinking of it since last evening with painful insistence.

"Your position then is," the Bishop demanded, "that this second miracle occurred apart from your will?"

"Yes," she replied. "I felt pity for the child, but I had no desire to cure her. I was not praying to God for her. As I was resting in Him, it was His will to silence an importuning mouth, and He quieted it through my voice."

Sister Lucinie noticed that Mother Cécile was again unhappy, torn from the moment of the first question, and with a gesture she calmed her sorrow.

"At the time of the first miracle you were acting independently of God?"

The nun heard the voice coming to her from a great distance and saw herself once more in that room in Morocco.

"Nobody obtains a complete independence ever. God allowed me to approve or to refuse, but He alone acted. I was free to the extent that a dog on a leash can eat,

202

drink, sleep, or prevent a stranger from entering, at will, but cannot go away."

She could hear her voice and reflected on her words, but a definite part of her soul was back again in the little community she had left, where she could see Sister Anne of the Cross seated beside Sister Dominique, their two faces clearly visible in the soft light of the parlor. She wanted their protection, and in spite of herself she turned to look once more at the Superiors who were present, seeking to find in their faces some reflection of the helpful affection she needed.

"Do you mean to say," the Bishop insisted, "that you could obtain any kind of miracle if you asked for it?"

Sister Lucinie hesitated. She had never put to herself such a question. She felt that it would be enough for her to wish and that God, who kept Himself so jealously in the unknown, would grant her as a mark of love, but even more as a test, this complete and uncontrolled power.

She recognized the danger, seeing the extent to which her union with God depended on herself, and the extent to which, within the precise limits of her independence as defined by the material part of her, she remained through submission to the divine will mistress of their common love. No tribunal could threaten her as much as her own choice. Her alarm came no longer from her judges or their power to punish her, but from her fear of making a mistake.

"It would be impossible for me," she said, "to do anything not pleasing to Our Lord."

She did not answer the Bishop but God Himself, realizing that He who was also an attentive and implacable judge was quite close to her and ready to enfold her.

"That being so," the little priest suggested casually, "could you not prove your power for us by some act of no significance but sufficiently extraordinary to compel our acceptance?"

Sister Lucinie stood straight up. Her face was bloodless and her hand raised in an appeal to God. The seven of them surrounded her like a carnival crowd in front of a sleight-of-hand performer.

"No," she groaned. She wanted desperately to get away, to shake off their suspicious disbelief, and to get close to God who sustained her only by imposing on her a perfection to which she did not feel the strength to aspire.

Her soul failed to make any contact. It was panicking under the offense. Suddenly she wanted to end her search so as not to tarnish it with bitterness, but the atmosphere remained full of the desired presence, denied under a recognizable form, vague, and nevertheless quite near. Sister Lucinie felt it as she felt the coolness of the room, the humidity that slowly was freeing her without her being aware of it, in the painful yearning after the unknown. Her tears were falling, burning her eyelids and her chest. That was not right. She did not want to offer anything except joy.

She did not see the Bishop coming toward her nor the Mothers Superior rising to their feet. The priest's voice soliciting a miracle still sounded in her ears, a little like a foolish child expecting that the doll in its silk dress will come alive and with a gesture change an orange into a carriage. He wanted a proof, not a proof of the sanctity and power of Sister Lucinie, but of the reality of God. The nun dwelt on the words, startled by their meaning, thinking herself guilty for having coupled them with His name, knowing how unworthy she still was in spite of God's choice which astonished her with an amazement and gratitude without limits. The priest asked for a miracle as a help or a prop on which to rest his soul, a remedy against the subconscious doubt in his mind. God had twice given such proofs through her means, and those who surrounded her still did not believe. Each of them called for a sign without knowing how to recognize all around the continuous renewal of the divine gesture.

"God," said Sister Lucinie in a loud voice, "established physical laws that we should obey and that should compel our daily wonder. We ask for the multiplication of the loaves without recognizing that every year in the obscurity of the earth the wheat renews millions of times Christ's gesture. A single germ suffices to create a hundred grains. To learn that, as the peasant or the scientist does, and with the same astonishment, is to serve God and help Him in His work with submission and intelligence, following His commandments. Do not look for Him in the unknown, but on the contrary look for Him humbly in law, wisdom, and the beauty of the rule."

Nevertheless, God had submitted His will to Sister Lucinie. She wondered in silence, removed from the rest of the group by her closed eyelids, alone in the tenderness that enfolded her. She had not asked for anything like this, but she had received the gift of passing beyond the laws that she wished to respect, or if this had not been given to her, it was permitted to her. Actually

205

she had done nothing. She loved God, and God had acted accordingly.

She smiled. She forgot the others and they, in the sight of the beautiful face in ecstasy, ceased their inquiry to follow the slow and sweet illumination. The three Mothers Superior surrounded the nun attentively, allowing the silent hour to flow past, fearful lest this excessively long period of contemplation might be too much for the frail young woman, suddenly startled to realize that she no longer belonged to them but was detached, still sharing life on earth yet carried beyond the limits of matter to a kingdom in which they believed but the approach of which they feared.

Sister Lucinie sighed. The Mother General took her hand which raised itself to seize something ungraspable.

"Daughter," she prayed.

The nun returned to life, reassured the women with a scarcely observable smile, and with a gesture invited the men to sit down again. She recalled that she was in the Bishop's presence, but the world's protocol no longer concerned her. The little gathering seemed to her to exist beyond her reach.

"My dear Sister Lucinie," said His Excellency, "our presence disturbs you. If tomorrow . . . "

Her cousin was also beside her. She heard him speak about his wife without being able to conjure up any image of her in her memory. They left.

She stood up. The Mother General opened a way for her and followed her to the blue courtyard where the fountain of water was singing. The nuns appeared at each doorway, watching from a distance the silent group on which the cool freshness of the evening was falling.

Sister Lucinie sighed again. It was no longer the novitiate or the little house from which she had recently come. These new faces turned toward her with fearful admiration, and the hesitation of their attitude respected her silence. She loved them and called to them while she still looked for God, and this double current of love toward the unknown and toward these tangible bodies gave her peace. Her companions approached, silent, smiling, their white faces hidden in the white shade of their cornettes. The community gathered around her again. Everyone wanted to protect and follow her, and already their hands were serving her.

Chapter XXV

T H E C E L L was bright in spite of the cast-iron lattice-work shading the window and the leaden sky heavy with rain over the tall minarets of the town. The gray light fell on the blue floor, but the lime-washed walls, the white bed, and the table of pale cedar, still perfumed with resin, lighted up the poor day.

"You see, Mother, her room is like ours and still it is different."

The two Mothers Superior paused on the doorstep between the silent calm of the room and the dull courtyard where the water pattered on the flagstones, raising spurts of foam. The covered gallery protected them only in part from the rain, yet they did not cross the doorstep, and spoke in low tones so as not to disturb the peace of the cell.

The Mother General studied each object.

"Yes," she answered, "such perfect order and the absence, in spite of meticulous correctness, of anything that might modify the cell in favor of its occupant. There is not even a rosary or a holy picture to give it a personal atmosphere."

A sense of awe obliged the two women to pause reflectingly between their words. Because of their heavy habits, they were not conscious of the humidity and the cold. Mother Madeleine made an ample gesture, which might be taken to indicate the bed, the window, or simply the empty space.

"Do you not think that God is there?"

Her voice fell to a muffled whisper that forced her companion to hold her ear almost against her companion's mouth.

"I have often asked myself why a sense of the divine presence makes itself felt in one place more than in another. At one time I used to think that the purpose of the building brought out this presence, and that the placing of the Blessed Sacrament necessarily produced it. But quite a long time ago, when I landed for the first time in North Africa, I went to pray in the cathedral in the town. It was an enormous building in Byzantine style, perched above an imposing flight of steps, under a golden and blue mosaic façade. The interior was magnificent, with light shining on the altar, light falling on the seats, and light penetrating even right into the confessionals. I did not *feel* God's presence."

209

A new meditative silence took possession of the dark forms, the starched headdresses all the while leaning toward each other, as if waiting for their thoughts.

"Nevertheless," Mother Madeleine remarked, "I thought that light was a symbol of God, and yet I did not find Him anywhere in that place. Do you not think that the proportions of the building might have an influence on its atmosphere?"

"No," the Mother General answered. "The harmony of the proportions is not a hindrance, but I do not think it indispensable. The size of the building makes no difference. The cathedral you are talking about is not so big as Notre Dame de Chartres and still you feel God there."

She hesitated for a moment. Her voice sounded louder than her companion's and the white wings of their cornettes moved apart.

"The illumination plays a part. God is light, but for us He hides Himself in darkness, and perhaps He prefers the places where men can guess at His presence only through the dusk. But all this reduces itself or can be reduced to a personal impression, and perhaps we feel God in a certain place not because He is really there but because our preconceived notion of His presence arouses in us a special emotion that we interpret in our own way."

Mother Madeleine listened to the Mother General reverently. Yet what the other said troubled her deeply. She accordingly took up the Mother General's last argument.

"I am unable to follow you on this road," she said. "One day when I was going through the native markets I stopped in front of a mosque and went inside. There was no question of light, for the markets are covered over with reed matting, and accordingly when I went into the temple I did not experience this change in the intensity of the light that may prepare the faithful for mystic emotions. The brightness of the day was the same inside as out. As all the doors were open, I had the impression of not even losing contact with the life of the little streets.

"Now this occurred at the beginning of my stay, during that period of complete certainty when I considered all non-Christians as God's enemies and when I imagined that the Lord did not visit their places of prayer. Nevertheless, I felt the presence of God in that spot. I do not mean to say that the communication was equal in intensity to that which Sister Lucinie receives. No, it was just an ordinary impression such as anybody can experience when going into a holy place that compels silence and recollection and respect, and which, at the same time, removes you from yourself because of the problems it creates for you and turns you inward on your soul through the reflection it demands."

The rain was now beating in on them and wetting the lower parts of their skirts, but they did not even notice.

"Do you suppose that recollection alone calls to our mind the thought of God?" the Mother General asked. "Nevertheless, I have been present at some Jewish religious ceremonies where there was no question of respect for the places in the way we expect, with measured gestures and words, and a desire to separate the profane strictly from the sacred. And still I recognized God there.

211

"In any place in which the masses pray He can be found. No doubt the massive appeal of these souls holds Him. I remember that by definition He exists everywhere, but in certain places He is indifferent and in others, on the contrary, attentive, and sometimes we can find Him far away from the churches, during a walk, in a particularly wild place, or, on the contrary, in a very quiet one."

Mother Madeleine summed up her thought in a louder voice. "An attentive presence," she repeated emphatically.

They were still standing in the same place, forgetting everything to study this white room. From time to time a nun passed near them, moving a little out into the rain so as not to bump into them, and casting an anxious look at the little cedar writing desk.

"You sent her to us for a little while, and now you are taking her away again," Mother Madeleine remarked. "You have no idea how important her action here has been."

She fell silent, expecting the Mother General to agree, but the latter merely stared at the ground without saying a word.

"We were losing our way," Mother Madeleine went on. "You cannot get the country out of your mind. Its luxury, cruelty, and aridity were entering our hearts. Her presence has swept all that away and accumulated in us a reserve of new strength. I wish you would stay until she has finished embroidering the altar cloth. That would remain as a tangible souvenir of her for us. Nevertheless, if you will forgive my saying so, I'd rather not keep her here with me after you leave. I wouldn't know how to deal with her."

"Why?"

Mother Madeleine hesitated before putting her thoughts into words.

"What do we know about others?" she asked. "What do we know about sanctity? St. Bernard was a saint and so was Bernadette Soubirous, but not by the same means; the one by knowledge and austerity and the other by a free gift of God. Who can tell us that Bernadette, if left to herself, would not have failed? She was protected by her convent, but we know that all the saints have been tempted. How many others, chosen at the beginning of their lives, let themselves go later on, and what a responsibility for those on whom they depend!"

The Mother General smiled ironically. She found in these words the same fears that Mother Cécile had expressed.

"You already are thinking of Sister Lucinie as a saint," she said, "and you are afraid to see her despoiled of her greatness. I do not think that is possible, or that God will never abandon her again. On the other hand, we cannot help or protect her. To maintain its value, her effort must remain hers alone."

"Nevertheless," Mother Madeleine insisted, "do you not think that the principal temptation that our Sister might fear would be that of pride and that in that respect at least we might be able by observance of the rule to keep her from slipping?"

The Mother General laughed so openly as to offend her companion.

"Mother Madeleine," she insisted, "you don't understand Sister Lucinie. She now lives at a level where we cannot reach her. There is room for pride in more humble attitudes, but not in her. At the beginning of her novitiate she could judge herself, just as she might have examined one of her companions, without introducing the notions of humility or pride that falsify our thoughts. We taught her to mistrust herself, and in doing so we fettered her impulse toward higher things. Now she has separated herself from our measures and she accepts the call."

She ceased speaking, took a long look at the room, and closed the door. The two women walked a few steps along the gallery and then paused again.

"Are you not afraid," Mother Madeleine suggested in a loud voice, "that her longing for God may not overcome her fear, and that she may leave us?"

The Mother General's happy laugh sounded out again in the rain, and Mother Madeleine was amazed anew. She never understood humor in serious matters. Nevertheless, her reverence and affection for the visitor prevented her from expressing her disapproval.

"Daughter, we all share the same anxiety. Why not admit that perhaps she may soon die? As you expressed it just now, the saints win their positions by different kinds of battles, but for her everything was easy. Her work, her virtue, and this final detachment that seemed so painful, all of that was accomplished in her without a struggle, as if only the body played a part and the soul had always been perfect. That is why I see in her an angel rather than a saint and why I anticipate her death."

A brief sob shook her. Mother Madeleine wept in silence, for the General's frankness allowed her pain to flow to the surface, and Sister Paule, who was passing, did not dare raise her eyes toward the two women.

The Mother General's remark soon spread through the convent, and each nun heard it with sorrow in her soul. All the October rain could flood from the ocean all the way to the town, weeping over the motley inhabitants and repeating its lamentation on the sidewalks; nothing could equal their sorrow.

"Nevertheless, she is still alive," the Mother General had gone on, "and we should make sure of future souvenirs for ourselves, for you this altar cloth which she is embroidering, for me the witness of her existence, and for all these others, my daughters, the favor of her example."

All the nuns had been gathering around for the past few minutes, a white and black group, all watching the water pouring down, as though a living source was irretrievably lost with it.

Chapter XXVI

AFTER the long rains the purified autumn rewarmed the town under a joyful sun. The community, assembled on the terrace, surrounded Sister Lucinie.

Sitting here, she could see the entire town with its innumerable even, white houses grouped around eight mosques with green cupolas rising in terraces on the slope of a hill. Farther off in the plain the brown stubble of the previous harvest, through which the first wild grasses of the new season were already pushing their tops, mixed the golds and greens of the vegetation with the purple and red colors of the earth.

Sister Lucinie embroidered with a sad weariness, caught up in her love as in an enchanted net, full of an unusual pity for herself, for this aching body that had to be encouraged and sustained through patience.

"Daughter," Mother Madeleine said, "our sisters would like to ask you for some advice before you leave."

The nun lay down her work and looked at the thin hand on which her ascetic way of life was written. The Superior's question interrupted her dream without succeeding in directing her toward another one. Mother Cécile touched her arm and then she looked up and saw the circle of wide-open serious eyes that formed a barrier around her.

"We should like to know," Sister Monique said, "if work is more important than prayer in our religious life."

Sister Lucinie hesitated.

"I believe that your rule is enough."

She turned anxiously toward the Mother General. Mother Cécile laid her fingers on those of Sister Lucinie. She still needed the friendship of others. The old nun's habitual mistrust had filled her with sorrow, but this gesture, so like that of Sister Anne of the Cross, finally harmonized their relations. Her heart did not withdraw from these women, nor did it strip itself of earthly affection. She loved this Sister Paule, this Monique with the sad eyes, this house with its lyrical fountain. She loved the hostile town and the widespread plain, these golds, these reds, this throbbing and dangerous land, ready for the attack, spread out in the sun like a sleeping wild beast.

"The rule is enough," the Mother General repeated approvingly, "but tell us about the direction in which your soul draws you. Explain to us what kind of prayers you use. Could you not clarify for us the rules of conduct which lead you toward God?"

Sister Lucinie was torn in two by the intellectual effort they all demanded of her, and by this appeal to the
inmost depths of her soul. She went toward God as He
came toward her, without knowing any more about the
structure of her longing than she did about the quality
of that of her true love.

"I do nothing special," she confessed. "You know just
as well as I do what are our common tasks. I do not
think that the quantity or the nature of the works or of
the prayers makes too much difference. Everything re-
volves around the quality of the act of will with which
we perform them. I cannot give you any clear instruc-
tions, for I have not worked out any formal techniques
designed to lead me toward God. I have moved toward
Him because He drew me."

She paused for a moment, admiring the flash and play
of light on the plain and the glassy brilliance of the
distant sun.

"I do not mean to say," she explained, "that I did not
try to reach God, but only that I did not hope to find
Him during this life. I offered Him my prayers and my
work, or rather the joy or sorrow involved in them, because as far as exertion itself was concerned, I forced
myself to distinguish and separate it from every idea of
salvation, to accomplish it and direct it to the greatest
perfection of its own purposes, because it contains in itself its own essentiality. I performed my social duties
because God created me to follow a human destiny. Only
the spiritual results returned to God, because He granted
them to me."

Her companions listened with deep emotion, but the
disappointment that her answer gave them was visible

on their faces. They had been hoping for an almost mathematical demonstration of sanctity, a mechanical dismantling of mysticism like that of a gymnastic exercise performed to music. Mother Cécile was watching them and thinking that nothing of this message would remain if nobody took the trouble to write down her words. She tried to recall them and recited mentally: "I tried to guide my exertions to the greatest perfection of their purposes, because they contain in themselves their own essentiality." The rest escaped her. She could remember only the sense.

The nuns remained silent, relaxing in the well-being of the autumnal warmth. They forgot Sister Lucinie to follow the movement of the pellucid clouds that drew together and moved apart in the sky like wool on a spinning wheel.

Sister Lucinie walked over to the parapet, and the Mothers Superior surrounded her with their constant care.

"I know nothing of God, but I love Him, and no matter what He may prove to be or what may be my destiny, I submit myself to Him."

The three elder women recorded the testimony in their minds. This act of faith alarmed them by its solemnity as well as by an emotional intensity quite foreign to Sister Lucinie's normal pattern of behavior. It seemed to them that by speaking thus in their presence she was summoning them as witnesses before an unknown tribunal.

The nun again saw the utter beauty of the countryside. Everything had become a lesson for her, as if each element offered her an instruction and confided a secret.

The material world seemed, as the days went by, to assume its own spirituality and to become endowed with a faculty of expression that Sister Lucinie had never previously known. The nun was still careful about drawing conclusions, but her fear of error had grown less. Any error in interpretation could not from now on separate her from God, whom she intuitively recognized under this diffused intelligence spread all about her. It was not a soul in the strict sense of the word but the Lord spread throughout the universe.

Sister Lucinie caught hold of the Mother General's arm. She understood with an overwhelming joy that God lived in her and was her soul. She understood, too, that her soul from the very beginning in the confused and awkward blindness of her search had identified itself in Him and had looked only for unity. Her fears and hesitations had come from her ignorance. She humbled herself in prayer, finally freed from effort, forgetful of her remorse, her body, and her life.

The wind ruffled her heavy skirt slightly and blew the black veil of her headdress against her cheeks. God rose up within her, lifting her soul out of her body, lingering in the happiness of reunion.